Sunnybank:

HOME OF LAD

Books by
ALBERT PAYSON TERHUNE

☉

☉

ALBERT PAYSON TERHUNE

Sunnybank:

HOME OF LAD

Grosset & Dunlap

PUBLISHERS

NEW YORK

To
THE MISTRESS
(*Sunnybank's Happy Debt to Her
is Almost as Great as Mine*)
*This Book
About Our Loved Home is
Dedicated*

☉

Contents

Sunnybank:

HOME OF LAD

CHAPTER ONE

Sunnybank

A BUSY highway cuts in two a tract of sweet primitive countryside that runs from the hinterland mountain forests down to the lake.

Forty acres of this bisected hill and woods and meadow and lakeside are mine; acres redeemed from the wilderness, seventy-odd years ago, by my parents, who gave their backwoods home the name, "Sunnybank."

By chance or by foresight, my father built Sunnybank House on a plateau a furlong below the trail which now is a well-paved roadway and atop a broad forest lawn that sloped to the lake. He laid out a meandering driveway through an oak-grove, from the trail to the plateau.

The house's timbers were of our native oak. Its beams, today, would turn an ax-edge. Folk built rock-solid in that era. I wonder how many modern abodes will stand the buffets of almost eighty years of blizzards and tornadoes and casual gales and the teeth of

1

rain and of snow, as stanchly as this rambling home of ours has stood them.

Those oak beams did more than form the framework for the house. Indirectly they led to the buying of Sunnybank.

My young father and mother were visiting in Pompton, a few miles from here. One afternoon they drove around the lake.

They had no thought of buying land or of building a home; especially in the wilderness more than twenty miles from their Newark base. Yet within an hour the land was bought.

It was one of those gorgeous impulses that shape life infinitely more than does all one's foursquare logical planning.

As they trotted along the woody trail my father brought the horses to a halt. He and my mother sat staring down through the oak-grown slope toward the lake. But each was watching a different scene.

My mother's eyes strayed over the gently dipping hillside grove to the plateau beneath and thence down a natural stretch of lawn to the shimmer of the sunset lake.

She found it inexpressibly beautiful. The shining green waterside lawn gave her the inspiration for naming the home she did not yet guess was to be hers.

My father was looking with greater intensity at something else on the hillside. And in his eyes and heart was hot indignation.

A gang of laborers were busy hacking down some of the gigantic oaks at the southern end of the slope. Evidently they had been at the desecrating job for days. For a big area of hillside had been cleared, and a strew of oak trunks lay everywhere.

To my father, as to myself in later years, there was something poignantly tragic in the slaying of a great tree. Something that sickened him to the very heart. Again and again I have heard him say:

"Any fool can cut down a mighty tree in half an hour. And Omnipotent God can't replace that tree in half a century."

Now, he was looking down at the wholesale assassination of grand oaks. Without stopping to reason that it was no concern of his and without so much as consulting my mother, he jumped to the ground and ran to where the men were chopping.

He asked the foreman of the gang the name and whereabouts of the land's owner. Then he gave the man a dollar to stop his choppers from working, until the owner could be located.

Half an hour later my parents had bought the whole menaced tract. It was the one way to check the orgy of tree-murder. Apart from that, the loveliness of The Place had wrought its magic on them.

A few weeks later, ground was broken on the plateau for the house's strong foundations. Laborers were hard at work hewing the fallen oak trunks into beams and joists.

That was the birth of Sunnybank; a home bought on illogical impulse and through a quixotic wish to save a forest from destruction.

Here on September second, 1906, my parents celebrated their golden wedding. Here on September second, 1926, the Mistress and I celebrated our silver wedding. The old house is as stanch today as in the year it was built.

But if oldtime North Jersey carpenters wrought for posterity, oldtime North Jersey painters seem to have had no such high ideals.

The house and the gate lodge and the barns and other outbuildings were done in French gray. The color was subdued and pretty. At least I have been told so. I never saw it.

For within a short time the gray peeled off, to the last flake. The priming beneath it was of far more enduring stuff. The priming was of a vivid wild-rose pink—a hell of a color for a house.

For some nineteen years thereafter, all the Sunnybank buildings blushed for the omission sins of their painters.

My first memory of The Place was of this shrill pinkness. Because it was the color of Sunnybank it seemed wholly beautiful to me, as did—and does—everything else connected with our home.

Why my parents did not change the awesome hue for some less horrible tint I don't know. They had good taste and they must have detested the coloring of the house they loved.

Perhaps they felt they could not afford the wholesale repainting. This, though they spent larger sums on things much less needful.

If so, I can understand their reasoning. I have inherited from them that eager willingness to spend more than I can afford, along certain lines; and to be worse than miserly in more important cash outlays. It is a human trait less uncommon than you may realize.

Whatever their reason, my parents left Sunnybank in its primal—or priming—pinkness for an unconscionably long time. Then during my boyhood it was painted a less hysterical color: a dingy chocolate somewhat vile to look upon.

Last of all it was stuccoed in gray. The stuccoing was done by me, soon after Sunnybank became ours in 1909.

My father was pastor of a church in Newark, New Jersey. On Sundays he made the twenty-mile journey back and forth behind two fast trotters.

Fast horses were his delight. He was a supreme horseman and an all-round athlete. One of his hardshell deacons took him to task for his taste in horseflesh. My father answered that he thought he could get to heaven as surely behind a fast horse as behind a slow one.

His new-bought land was part of a crown grant bestowed in 1695 on one Arent Schuyler. The tract ran east and west for many a rolling mile of woodland and lake and mountain and stream, throughout the southern end of the Ramapo Valley.

Its borderline was indicated by twisting oak saplings, twined into fantastic shapes.

A score of these trees—now about two hundred

and forty years old—still stand at Sunnybank. I have traced the course of a hundred more for miles back through the hills. Several of them have rotted or have been blown down, in my own time. They look as though Albrecht Dürer had designed them.

Near the lake and to the south of the house was a meadow overgrown with brambles. My father set his men to work clearing and draining this for an orchard. A foot or two underground they came upon a few rotted shreds of blue cloth and some eartheaten bones.

Alongside these grisly relics lay a sheathed sword. The years had turned the scabbard into friable rust. But the scabbard had protected the sword inside it.

My father made inquiries. He found Lieutenant-Colonel Van Cortlandt's Revolutionary regiment had encamped there during the cruel winter of 1777–1778. (A "regiment" in the Continental army just then was any body of men, from one hundred up.) An officer of note had died of "the lung fever"—pneumonia—during that ghastly winter. He had been buried with military honors. These honors included his sidearms.

Our Revolutionary army had few swords, except those captured from the British. Thus it must have caused a wrench to allow one of the prized weapons to be interred with its dead wearer. Beneath the hilt of the retrieved sword was the insignia of a British engineer regiment.

My father had the decaying bones buried in consecrated ground. The sword hangs today on the mellowed brick chimney piece above my living room fireplace. Only a few hundred yards from where its owner was buried. It is a mute link between the present and the far past of Sunnybank.

Our state of New Jersey was a dark and bloody ground throughout the long years of the Revolution. American and British armies fought across and across it, year after year. Washington slept in numberless old North Jersey houses—what an inveterate slumberer he must have been!—and Revolutionary relics have been turned up in hundreds, by plowshare and spade.

Back in the Ramapo hills, for example, I found a rusted cannonball that during the Revolution had been jostled from a heavy-laden cart driven stealthily by night along the hidden "Cannon Ball Road," whose lower outlet is a bare mile from Sunnybank.

And high in the Ramapo Mountains I came across a pair of Hessian handcuffs. Did their fugitive wearer die in them, and was his body rotted to earthy mold, leaving only this sign of his captivity? Or did he slip free of them when hunger made his wrists thin? I wish I might know.

In any event, cannonball and handcuffs are still here at Sunnybank, along with the blackened sword. In my childhood, too, there were rough cairns whereunder slept Continental soldiers who had died or been killed near here.

My father told me that in his first years on The Place there were oldsters who still spoke familiarly of "Mister Washington," whom their own parents

had seen more than once on his rides to and from
Morristown.

Always they used the prefix, "Mister," in speaking
of him. They had numberless anecdotes to tell of
Washington; some dull enough to be true, others
patently fantastic.

There were Indian villages and encampments, here,
before the invasion of the Dutch. Many an arrowhead
has been turned up by Sunnybank plows. A few rude
stone utensils and the like have been found here, too.

Most of the old houses of any pretensions, in my
childhood, still had the "slave quarters" in their back
gardens; rotting souvenirs of the days before New
Jersey found slave-holding unprofitable and abolished it.

Yes, this is historic ground; now wholly surrounded
by commuters and the like. Peace to a dead past!

I was nearly twenty years old before the commuter
came. There were not two other houses within a mile
of ours. The lake was full of fish. The forests were
rife with game. Time had stood still for this sweet
hinterland.

In several churches within an eight-mile radius
services were held in Dutch, as they had been held for
two hundred years past.

My father spoke Dutch fairly well. It was the language of his ancestors in the centuries before quar-
relsome old Albert Albertse Terhune founded the
family in America in 1642.

I do not speak a word of it.

I was made to feel woefully illiterate, more than

once, during school and college years, when I dropped in for a meal at some farmhouse on a hunting trip and when my rustic host told a story whose point was in Dutch.

Even the farmhands at the clothless table yelped with laughter. And I had not understood a syllable.

At Bog Und Vlei, at the very bottom of the long and winding Ramapo Valley, dwelt a rich old farmer who looked like Michaelangelo's Moses the Lawgiver. Except for the latter's horns. Folk said the oldster's young fourth wife had supplied him right plentifully with these. But they were invisible.

He spoke no word of English. In my early boyhood my father and I stopped to see him while we were on one of our long horseback rides. The two men talked together in Dutch. In the course of the chat the farmer said he had been laughed at for not taking the trouble to learn English. He explained:

"Why should I bother to study a newfangled language that's never going to be spoken to any extent around here? In North Jersey a knowledge of Dutch will always take me anywhere."

There are still one or two churches in that same eight-mile radius where service and sermon are carried on in Dutch. But it is Greek to ninety-five per cent of the present-day Jerseymen.

When I was a boy there were many odd phrases and expressions that dotted the speech of the now-forgotten oldtimers. These words may or may not have had Dutch origin.

"Bitter" was used as a synonym for intently. As "You was a walkin' bitter," and "He eyed me bitter," and "They loved one the other bitter."

"A wee peckle" was used to denote any very small quantity. "Snide" meant cut. "Drug" was used for dragged. "That's been it" was the almost universal form of that was it, and for that's true. A favorite term of astonishment or of admiration was "Mythuh! Mythuh!"

All this in my youth. You will listen long, before you hear any of these expressions—or a hundred like them—nowadays. Local language, except among the Jackson Whites survivors, is as correctly modern as is the concrete highroad that passes The Place.

In the early 1890's, the commuter came. So did the powder works. The gracious frontier vanished.

A village and mills—the powder houses were scenes of occasional devastating explosions—sprang up overnight in the woods and meadows across our lake where I had shot quail. But on the Sunnybank side of the lake, a very few of us have been able to keep two miles or more of the pleasant country as it was.

"They shall not pass!" has been our war cry. Except for the oft-mentioned concrete road and the swarm of motorists it entails, we have been able to hold our own against the inroads of progress.

Of course, it is only a matter of time until our hard-held barriers must crash. Only for a pitiably short while can the past hope to hold back the present. But during that space, Sunnybank remains Sunnybank. And

two miles or so of eastern lake front are as they used
to be.

On the friendly green banks of the lake, opposite
us and less than a mile away, roadhouses have been
opened, with fleets of livery boats and a swimming
beach as added attractions. Hordes of motorists are
drawn to them; and thence out into the lake either
to fish or for a swim.

My nephew, Frederic F. Van de Water, one of the
wisest men I have known, has described these hordes
right inspiredly as "tent caterpillars."

They strip foliage and leave the once-bright greensward of the lake's verge an expanse of hard-trodden
clay.

Incidentally, their mirthful howls and songs smash
the soft silences of the lake almost as distressingly as do
the two roaring and sputtering livery motor speed
boats which circle the waters on Sundays and on holi-
days.

The fish are fewer each year, thanks to the navy of
livery rowboats and to the charming unsportsmanliness
of some of their imported occupants.

I was told of one such fisherman who boasted loudly
that he and three friends had caught seventy-two black
bass in Pompton Lake, in a single fourteen-hour day;
and of another boatload crew who admitted catching
eighty-four pickerel in the same space of time.

Why not use dynamite and make a clean job of the
slaughter?

Nearly every accessible lake within easy motor ride

of a big city has like misfortune. I realize that the urban motorist has the right to defile everything within his reach. But bit by bit he is wrecking his own sport. He is wiping out the very things which draw him to the back country, fish, blossoms, woods, grass, forest game, and the mystic hush of the hills!

My father was loved, hereabouts, during his half century of sojourn in the Pomptons. More, he was trusted. People brought their troubles to him. They accepted his counsel.

Even the lawless Jackson Whites far back among the Ramapo Hills let him hunt through their sinister country unmolested, knowing he would bring home no tales of liquor stills and caches and other mountain secrets.

Because of him, they gave me the same queer immunity during my hunting and hiking days. I blundered upon more than one such "mountain secret" on those long-ago hunts of mine. And I kept my mouth shut.

As far back as I can remember, The Place has had a grip on me that I can't explain. It is the only spot on earth where I want to live. Every tree, every foot of its rolling wooded acres is inexpressibly dear to me. So is the fire-blue lake at the bottom of the lawn, with the green miles of hills that encircle it.

To me there is a nameless spell about it all; a fulfillment of the pre-Revolutionary Pompton saying:

"No one who has been caught by the magic of these hills can stay long away from them."

This may be sloppy nonsense, for all I know. My

saner self tells me there are fifty regions more beautiful than this; and that Sunnybank itself has little in common with the show places I have visited or with countless historic beauty spots.

Your saner self tells you your sweetheart or wife or child or mother cannot compare in looks or intellect or charm with a hundred other women and children you have seen. But your heart is wise enough to give your saner self the lie.

Let it go at that.

Just the same, there *is* a peace and a loveliness about The Place.

There is a something which we who live here and who love The Place so deeply have not been able to analyze. That nameless something has touched other people besides ourselves. Not necessarily our intimate friends, but those who need comfort.

There was a woman—beautiful, brilliant, high-bred —wasting fast from a black malady she knew was mortal—who used to drive here whenever she was able to leave her bed. She said to us on one visit:

"There is a strange peace that comes over me the instant my car turns into your gateway and down the drive." (Others have told us the same thing.) "It helps me to carry on for days afterwards. Won't you let me rest for an hour or so on your big living room couch and look out through the wistaria vines and listen to a little Chopin? If you will, the peace will stay longer with me. It will give me something to hold onto in the nights that are so endless."

A *gallant* woman, who won her life-fight by losing it.

Another friend—a hard-headed business man whom I had not seen in years—came for an hour's chat, not long ago. We were talking aimlessly about old times when he broke off in the middle of a sentence to ask me:

"Do you believe the dead come back to those of us who can't forget them?"

"One can only hope so," I stammered, confused by such a question from such a man. "Why?"

"Because," he made shamefaced answer, as if against his will, "there is a something about Sunnybank—I felt it even when I was a child—that makes me—that—. In the years since my sweet wife died, I have longed unspeakably to have some sign that she hadn't gone from me for always. It never came to me till a few minutes ago. Now I feel as if—as if she were right here with me. If our dead can come back to us, surely it is here they would come."

Absurd, isn't it?

Besides, there are at least two people among our friends—a man and a woman who never have met—who frankly are bored by Sunnybank and who condole with us on the monotony which must be ours after our dual day's work is ended. They tell us, indirectly, that life must be a ghastly bore, a drab dullness, during our golden leisure hours here. (We who find our Sunnybank days so short!)

There are several others to whom our home does not appeal.

So there is diversity of opinion. For which we care

not in the least. It is Sunnybank. It is the place where both the Mistress and I are happy—thanks to the Mistress.

The spell—if there be a spell—was summed up best, I think, by a somewhat abhorrent person who came out here to see me on business a few years ago.

He was a sub-Babbitt, a man of vast waistline and of flaring and dazzling raiment, a rich city dweller of sweatshop origin.

Puzzled, he roamed about the house and the grounds. Ever his fat face grew more puckered with perplexity. At last he wheeled on the Mistress and myself, growling with something like accusation:

"What is there to Sunnybank that makes me feel this funny way? It don't spell money. It don't spell style. But—Lord, something about it kind of GETS me!"

Less convincingly, too gushingly, a magazine writer sought to describe it, after a visit here:

"There were woods running down from the road —just woods. Not a dinky park. And a drive wound down through them, a furlong or so, to a gray old stucco house with dark woodwork and with wistaria all over it and a comfy green barn set back in the trees.

"There was a glorious big collie asleep on the steps, and there were glowing flowers in tubs and boxes on the gray veranda, and flowers and vines everywhere and stretches of shade-dappled grass.

"Then from the house a great lawn sloped down to the lake—about another hundred and fifty yards. There were huge old oaks on the lawn, too, and evergreen trees, and there was a rustic boathouse in the cove to one side.

"The lawn was on a kind of point that ran out into the lake; and all around the lake were soft green hills with bluish mountains beyond. They circled The Place as if they loved it and as if they were guarding it from harm.

"The sun was setting. It was setting over the other side of the lake. There were wonderful long shadows stretching up across the lawns. The dear old house was bathed in amber glow. That was the House of Peace, if ever there was one.

"And down to the left, close by the lake, there was a line of weeping willow trees. They were trailing their leaves into the blue water. Over the whole Place a strange light seemed to hover just then. Perhaps it was only the sunset. Or perhaps—perhaps it was the blessing of God!"

I make no apology for quoting this rhapsodic word picture. To me, it is Sunnybank, to the life. To you or to most normal mortals, Sunnybank may be just another of those commonplace little country homes.

I am not interested in convincing you it is anything more than that. It is a home. *Our* home.

CHAPTER TWO

Sunnybank Seasons

PERHAPS I am not a true devotee of the country, after all. I know people who ask nothing better than to live in it throughout the twelve months. To me, from early February to early April, it is a loathsome place. Even more so then than during the dead time from mid-November until the first snow.

By February, I and every other normal mortal should have had our fill of winter. The rest of it is dismal excess luggage. The eternal snow has lost all its novelty, all its exhilaration, all its beauty. The cold stops thrilling and begins to hurt.

Next come the soggy days when the snow leaves bare the gray grass and the ground gives a false promise of spring. In spite of a lifetime's experience I believe then that winter is at last on his way out.

I believe it until I wake some morning to a fresh snowfall several inches deep and to near-zero weather. And the whole dreary waiting has to begin all over again.

Along in March, early or late, the snow says good-bye except for a foolish flurry or two whose gigantic flakes stick to the sides of trees.

And worse sets in. Thawing days and freezing nights. Slowly, slimily, the frost begins to crawl out of the ground, making Sunnybank a foul quagmire.

It is spring's sorry advance notice. Its one redeeming feature is a song sparrow that wakes me in the morning amid the dribble of wet eaves or the hammer of March rain on the roof.

Through the vileness of the weather he sings a gloriously triumphant announcement that spring is here. Which it is not. But I bless him, none the less, for his optimism. Groundless optimism is so much more bearable in a bird than in a human.

The grass remains dust-gray and the wet air breeds a golden argosy of snuffles and the earth is rotted. Mud takes on all the worst features of mucilage. Cross-country walks are a sticky burden.

But the song sparrow can see farther into the murk than I can. He keeps on insisting that winter is gone and that the dead world is nearing resurrection.

At Sunnybank, the song sparrow's floral counterpart—coming to life around the tenth of April—is the purplish anemone, which is no anemone at all but a hepatica. The true anemone waits prudently until the earth once more is fit to bloom in.

In a dozen parts of the woods, between the house and the highway, I know where to find the clumps of low-growing hepatica, with furry dark green leaves trying to smother them.

Then I know the yearly miracle at long last is at

hand. The dogtooth violet and its fairer blue sister are on the way to us. The other early woodflowers are going to follow in swift succession. The skunk cabbage will stop looking like a greenish wart and will put out its flare of overpraised leaves. The willows will follow suit.

The hills will take on a pink hue. The pink will merge into faint green.

There is always one night in April when spring comes across the mountains to us.

You can tell that night by the smell and the feel of it. You can tell it, too, by the high-pitched sleighbell chorus of the frogs along the shore—an unearthly beautiful sound—and by the quacked conferences of the northbound ducks resting far out on the lake.

After that, there is no turning back of the miracle, however often it may be checked for the moment by killing frosts or by days of bitter wind or of downpouring rain. Always it advances, crashing through every obstacle; up to the climax of the pink-white seas of appleblossoms and the hanging avalanches of wistaria and the glory of tulips.

And the first gay flight of mosquitoes.

It is odd, this universal craving for the birth of spring. It is as rife among townsfolk as among us rustics; if one may judge from the land office business done by florists, in forced spring flowers.

I think the spring-yearning became a human instinct as far back as the day when the tusked Neanderthal man found his body no longer racked by cold and found he could shamble forth through snowless wastes to get the flesh food and the herbage he had missed so sorely during the prison months of winter.

From poets down—or up—spring has been press-agented past all belief. It has been hailed as a season of unbroken loveliness and of balmy air and of every other form of perfection.

It is nothing of the kind.

Even as we remember the picnics and not the tooth-aches of early youth, so we remember only the occasional divine days of springtime and we forget the inexcusably damnable weather of more than half of it. The Spaniards have an ancient proverb:

"May gives ten days to the killing of old people and cattle."

That is an understatement. As a rule, May allots more than ten days to weather such as neither old people nor cattle should care to live through. So does late April.

But it is human nature to recall only the wonders of a flashy product and to forget its drawbacks. Other-wise the stock exchange would close tomorrow for lack of once-bitten suckers.

Decades ago, in the newspaper game, my work and my inclinations threw me often into the comradeship of a tough little East Sider to whose words of wisdom I used to listen with more or less profit.

His dissertation upon spring is fresh in my memory. It is worth your reading. For it summed up that super-lauded season infinitely better than can any clumsy writing of mine.

On a prematurely warm March evening he and I foregathered at a prizefight. On our way home I made the brilliant forecast:

"Well, spring is coming."

He snorted in disdain. Then he loosed the vials of his wrath upon the approaching season and upon me.

"Sure, spring is coming!" he scoffed. "What the hell else would it do? What other direction is there for it to travel in? And when it gets here, what then? Hey? Tell me that?"

Before I could mumble something about the joys of violets and bock beer and open trolley cars, he was launched irefully on his theme.

I had him started. And I was sorry. For I did not want the sordid truth to blur the *frühlingsglaube* and my homesick visions of the misty green and pink of my Ramapo Hills and the first tender life of the Sunnybank lawns and woods.

But the little thug was as easy to start as trouble and as hard to stop. All unknowingly I had laid bare one of his philosophy veins. There was nothing for me to do but sit tight until it should be worked empty.

"Sure spring is coming!" he reiterated. "There's nothing else for the lousy old faker to do. Since P. T. Barnum, there's never been such another fourflushing public service humbuggist as that same Gentle Spring you're blatting about. It's always been pressagenting itself and inciting otherwise sane guys into poetical fits and offkey singing.

"Spring hands out more promises than all four of

the seasons could make good on. And it makes good on fewer of them than any of the other three. That's why it scores such a hit everywhere.

"It isn't what folks *do* that counts. It's what they make the world think they're *going* to do. Like spring, f'r instance. And politicians.

"Was there ever a circus that lived halfway up to its posters? And circuses are the most popular pests on earth.

"The Garden of Eden would look like an ashdump, alongside to a commuter's flower borders; if flowers was anywheres near a millionth as grand as their pictures in the seed catalogues. Yet more folks buy flower seeds every year.

"And spring is the champion heavyweight promiser of the whole outfit. It promises us everything. Except colds and malaria and ptomaine. And those three pretty gifts are the only things it's dead sure to bring us."

He paused for a moment. I could not think of any bright repartee. Then, speaking at first with a shamed hesitation that changed back into his wonted rapid-fire delivery as he went on, he said:

"I was batty about a girl, once. No, I wasn't, neither. I was in *love* with her. We were going to make it a case of matrimony. Then she up and died. A long while ago, it was. She said to me, just—just before:

" 'I'm going to be took back home to Jersey to be buried. Don't go to the funeral. It's all snowy and ugly in the country now. But come out to my grave, once, in the spring. It'll be all soft green and there'll be violets blooming on it and the birds will be singing in the sunset. It'll be sweeter for you to remember me that way.'

"So I waits till spring. Like she'd asked me to. Then I went there. Early in May, it was.

"It was raining like blue hell. And her grave, and all around it, was a muck of yellow clay with not a spear of grass within six feet. And there was a yellow puddle with a toad in it, where the headstone ought to of been.

"I got my feet soaked. And some measly commuter stole my silver-handled umbrella, coming back to town. Spring? *Gawd!*"

In his way he was right. But there is a catch in it somewhere. When Spring laughs, she has the stark magic to make one forget her foul temper.

Speaking of magic, I am certain that elves and pixies were invented by the first human who wandered alone, deep in a moonlit forest, late at night in spring. On such nights everything seems true. Except possibly the truth. And when spring and truth clash, truth must go by the board.

From mid-April on until the latest of late autumn, Sunnybank holds for me everything in nature. The riot of June roses, the waves of windswept grain, the smell of new hay, the first gallant red leaf that waves its futile "No surrender" flag at oncoming frost.

I have been told October is the crowning month of the year. To me it is not. It is beautiful. But it is infinitely sad. It foretells the death of things.

The killing hand already is on nature. Flaunt its gay banners as it will, the foliage knows it is doomed. So do the few fall flowers that have been able to stand up against the first frosts.

But there is infinitely more pathos in the pre-frost smiling hush of late September, the season when all nature is waiting so bravely for death.

The air is warm. Time stands still. There are a million flowers abloom. For days this goes on. Unafraid the blossoms wait. They and the weather seem to be trying to make up to us for what is to come so soon. Smiling, they face the fast-nearing frost.

I may be foolishly imaginative in this feeling of mine about late September. I should like to think I am. For it would rid me of a bit of a heartache.

Step by step the ever-recurring hard and harder frosts drive all life back into the earth; whither they follow it, closing the egress with a flinty floor. The last fleck of green is frozen from the sere grass. And a dead landscape waits for burial; as so lately a doomed landscape waited smiling for death.

I was laughed at right heartily when I was little for saying the trees fly south with the birds, leaving their lifeless nests of trunk and twig. But I have said foolisher things; even in this book.

The chilly fog and wet rot of November—darkest month of the year, photographers say—then the awesome white cold of winter. The snow scratching at the window panes, the wind howling across the lake from the dead white mountains beyond, the rifle-crack of miles of splitting ice and the anguished groan of air caught under the expanse of ice-sheet.

It is well, on evenings in early winter, to sit deep in a couch in front of a roaring hearth fire, at Sunnybank, reading, smoking, loafing, with collies sprawled asleep at one's feet, and listening to the yell of the gale against the stanch old house and through the naked giant oaks outside.

It is well to plow through drifts, with the dawn wind in one's eyes and a rackety swirl of dogs breaking the trail ahead.

But by February these things begin not only to pall on me, but to sicken me to the very marrow. And there comes to me the world-old yearning for distant spring, for the yearly miracle that seems so hopelessly far away.

Every April for the past quarter century I have been planting trees—scores of them a year—all over Sunnybank.

Fruit trees to eke out the seventy-five-year-old orchard's gaps. Trees for woods and groves and lawns, to help fill up the direful blank spaces left by the chestnut blight—a blight which wiped out nearly one hundred and twenty grand old trees on Sunnybank's forty acres alone,—new shade and forest trees; trees of every sort and description.

Oh, some of them are tediously slow in the growing! Oak saplings that I planted in 1910 are barely worth the name of adult trees today. Tulip poplars have shot up, tall, graceful, far-arching; those of them the scale has not stripped to corpses. Maples, some of them, have risen to fair size; while other varieties of them are snailic in their growth.

Hemlocks—slowest to grow of any of my plantings —still are spindly and ragged. Blue spruces have done much better. The Siberian elms have soared dizzily— except where they have dwindled and become dwarfed.

Locusts have thriven. They have sent up new shoots, mangrove-like, fifty feet from the parent trunk, forming little groves of fast-growing baby trees; fragrant— poignantly fragrant—on May nights with their wis- taria-like blooms.

Elms have made haste slowly; their pacemaker my seventeenth century patriarch elm whose base has a diameter of seven feet. Dogwood has bourgeoned al- most fastest of all; its white tents pitched showily on lawn and at woodland border.

Hard and vainly I fought to stem the murderous chestnut blight. From the rotted stumps of the dis- ease-slain chestnut trees a new crop of runners has sprung up, year after year. These runners I have cosseted in every way. Sometimes they rise to a height of fifteen feet, and bear a handful of chestnut burrs.

I have read that the nuts borne by these survivors are immune to the blight. So I save them and I plant them. Nothing comes up. I have sent far to buy new nuts and I have planted them with tender care in every type of soil Sunnybank can boast. Always the same negative result.

The runners spring up from the ancient roots. In

any time from a year to three years a dirty brown line encircles their lower stems. Then they die.

But I keep on with my fight to bring back the lost chestnut trees. I shall fail. But it is a good fight and worth losing.

Back in 1901, I have been told, a cargo of Japanese timber was delivered to the Bronx Zoo. The timber was alive with chestnut blight—whatever that blight may be. And with it there was no counter-blight to kill the germs.

So the malady spread, with nothing to check it. In every direction it traveled. I doubt if there are any healthy chestnut trees within seventy miles of New York today.

One by one our Sunnybank chestnuts died, great trees that had lived for a hundred years or more. I wrote to the government's forestry department for aid and advice. So did other people. That is all the good it did us.

This past year I have planted more than a hundred trees of various kinds; besides dozens of shrubs.

Why in the name of all that is sensible did I do such a futile thing? I am sixty-one years old. The Mistress is only a few years younger.

What possible benefit can she and I hope to derive from the planting of trees which will take from twenty to seventy years to reach full maturity?

That is a rhetorical question. There is no answer to it.

When she and I shall be dead, there is nobody who will care to carry on. Nobody with our fanatic adoration for our home and for every inch of our land. There is nobody who will have our foolish love of The Place and our desire to keep it up and to plant for the future.

Alien hands will hew down the mighty trees which mean so ineffably much to us. The Place will be cut up into dinky bungalow development lots—"attractive lake shore residence sites"—or it will be sold at a bargain for a hot dog Pleasure Park or for an inn.

Or, with the sign, "*Tourists Accommodated*," on its ancient stone gateposts, this house which was built into a shrine by my gentle mother and then by my gentler wife, will be turned over to the motor tourist.

Again calling sanity to my aid, I realize it cannot matter either to the Mistress or to myself what may happen to Sunnybank after we fall asleep. Yet—

I wish I had a living son to carry on. A son who would have inherited our stark Sunnybank complex. I wish with all my soul there were someone who might feel as the Mistress and I feel about the loved old homestead and carry on our manner of life here.

While we shall live, the Mistress and I shall plant. Not through any noble motive, but on the blind vital urge that makes a dying tree put forth a brave show of leaves in the spring of its last year of life.

On the principle which made my friend, Cap'n Bob Bartlett, start Chopin's "Funeral March" upon his cabin victrola as his ship, *The Karluk*, was beginning to sink.

A gesture, perhaps. Or perhaps something a trillion times greater. Who can say?

CHAPTER THREE

Indoors

THE old house has no definite architecture except of pleasant comfort. It had some eleven rooms when it was built. Then, as more children and more money drifted in, my parents made the house larger. A room here and a wing there. Until now it has sixteen rooms, only one or two of them large; one or two perhaps unduly small.

The beamed living room and the music room, I suppose, are one L-shaped room, divided as they are by an arch that goes almost from wall to wall.

We like the living room. So do most of our guests, they tell us. One or two people do not. The wide fireplace's brick mantel and chimney piece rise to the ceiling. In front of the fire is the only couch in captivity long enough for me to stretch out to the full extent of my six-feet-two-and-a-half-inches. The Mistress had it made for me.

It is nine feet long, over all, and with a seven-foot

resting space between the overstuffed ends. It is nearly a foot deeper, too, than the average couch. One sinks into it with vast sense of well-being.

It is dark brown. Brown is the general tone of the whole living room, for that matter, from the ancient Heppelwhite and Adam and Chippendale chairs and Sheraton desk—all handed down for God-knows-how-long in the Mistress's family—to the floor-to-ceiling clock which ticked out the hour of my great-grandsire's birth. It is a mellow room. A room that seems to me to to be full of peace.

The firelight is reflected from the rows of silver trophies at one side of the brown wooden walls and from a heterogeneous mass of old weapons and armor on the wall behind the couch. On three sides of the room are built-in bookshelves reaching from the floor to the high diamond-paned windows. The books range from quaint calf-bound volumes and sets, of our grand-parents' time, to the New Oxford Dictionary and the Cambridge Shakespeare.

Ours is a house of books, every room and every hallway of it. Books that are more friendly than valuable, for the most part.

In a corner of the living room above a reading bench are my "goodnight" shelves. I have given them this name because years ago when I had a long spell of insomnia I hit on a book cure for my pestilent sleeplessness.

I used to work during all or part of the evenings, in those days. I still do, at times. When I had finished, my alleged brain was flaringly wakeful. So, for an hour before I went to bed, I would lounge on this reading bench or on the couch, and read; to the accompaniment of at least two successive strong cigars and a bottle of ale.

I chose books I liked and which I had read over and over again. Thus I could open any one of them at whatsoever place I might choose and start in on my quiet hour. A queer mixture of literature those goodnight shelves hold:

All of Barrie's plays, my Shakespeare set, *The Three Musketeers*, *Pride and Prejudice* and *Sense and Sensibility*, *Barchester Towers*, a scatter of Thackeray and Dickens and Bret Harte, *Ingoldsby Legends*, two of F. P. A.'s rereadablest verse books, the Bible, some of Stevenson, some of Kipling, *Percy's Reliques*, *Guy Livingstone*, *Babbitt* and a tumble of other volumes.

A mixed lot, as you see. But any one of them can catch and hold my interest for all or part of my hour of pre-bedtime reading and can bring me forgetfulness of the work that has stirred me up, and make me ready for sleep. I never read a new book or a book I don't revel in, during that hour.

I am a crank on the subject of antique or strange weapons. For nearly forty years I have been collecting them, slowly and at intervals, in many parts of the world. I am much more of an enthusiast than an expert along this line. But I have picked up a few things that are good.

Among them is a Malay kreese whose wavy

brownish blade is sharp enough to shave with and on whose hilt are carved two cabalistic prayers—one that the wielder may win his fight, the other that the wound inflicted may be wide enough and deep enough to let the victim's soul escape through it to bliss.

Then there is a kittar—or khuttar, if you prefer. Its hilt is made up of two long vertical bars of inlaid steel, far enough apart to admit the hand and let it grip two crossbars an inch apart. Press these cross-bars together and the broad blade splits into three blades, all of them razor-sharp and needle-pointed.

I have read that one is supposed to stab without pressing the crossbars; then when the thrust has gone deep enough, to press the bars and twist the weapon all the way around. (Which may or may not have bred the first idea of making hamburg steak.)

Perhaps the most worth-while item in my mixed collection is a fifteenth century "Misericordia dagger" or dagger of mercy. You have read of such daggers in Froissart and in Scott. They could pierce the narrow joints of proof armor when a two-handed sword's thicker point could not.

Mercy dagger in hand, at tournaments, the victor would stand above his collapsed foe and would look to the royal dais for further orders.

In battle a mortally wounded warrior would stick its point into the bloody earth before him; its hilt and straight blade and the inordinately wide guard giving it the aspect of a cross. Or a comrade could lift it by the point and hold the cruciform weapon in front of a dying knight's eyes.

A very ancient and more than rare "India parrying dagger"—a museum piece—was given me long ago. A yellow ivory hilt has long kreese-like blades extending from each end of it. From its middle protrudes a short and squat and serrated blade that sticks out at right angles to the long curved blades.

This thing is a gem. Never before have I seen one, and once only have I come across a mention of it in any of my scant reading on the subject of rare weapons. Yet always it has puzzled me.

How in blazes was it used in a fight? Did its owner slash right and left with the keen longer blades and use the fat little serrated central blade for parrying? Or was it the other way around? I should be deep in the debt of anyone who knew and would explain to me.

In Scotland I was able to find a guaranteed and proven set of Highlander hand weapons dating back to Bonnie Prince Charlie's invasion of 1745. But never could I lay hands on a genuine targe, within my means, to make up the set.

As you may know, the clansmen went into battle carrying the long basket-hilt claymore in the right hand, the dirk in the left—the left arm which was guarded by the bull's hide targe or shield—and with a nasty little cairngorm topped knifelet stuck into the top of the sock or boot.

The dirk, perhaps eighteen inches long, had a scabbard in which were half-hidden a tiny two-tined fork and a table knife. This for use on campaigns.

For a dirk was semi-sacrosanct to the true Highlander. Like the kreese, it must have but two sheaths —its own and the body of its master's foe. It could not be desecrated by the cutting up of meat and the spreading of bread-and-cheese. Hence the utilitarian little knife-and-fork fastened into the scabbard.

The short dagger carried in the boot top or sock was a veritable toad among weapons. Its technical name was "sgian dhu" (black dagger). When a clansman was beaten to the ground by a stronger opponent or when he knelt for mercy, he could reach into his sock for the sgian dhu and drive it upward into his conqueror's abdomen. A pleasing trick, and sportmanlike withal.

The steel of my claymore and my dirk and my sgian dhu—like the steel of my Misericordia dagger —is of the half-luminous gray hue which only a century or more of rustless life can give to tempered steel.

The central object in the clutter of arms and the like, on the wall opposite the chimney piece, is a cuirass-and-tassets, from the Tower of London. Like the old weapons it is luminously gray. So is the lobster-tail Cromwellian helmet that tops it.

I have noticed an odd feature of those ancient English helmets. The wearer's face may be left wide-exposed to bullet or to blade. But the ears are almost invariably protected by hinged steel flaps. Apparently the ear was better worth guarding than were the eyes

or any of the rest of the face. I have read the reason
for this. I pass it on to you, though I have no proof it is
true.

In early England certain of the more disreputable
crimes and misdemeanors were punished by cropping
off the offender's ears. Sheep-stealing, poaching, and
far more degrading misdeeds. "Crop eared" was an
epithet of black insult.

Thus when a homecoming soldier arrived in his
native village, earless, he had vast difficulty in per-
suading the neighbors that his ears had been sliced
off by a French broadsword in the service of his
country, and that they had not been amputated by
the common hangman as penalty for some foul fault.
Hence the exaggerated care in guarding them.

Among my pistols on that wall are some dating
back for several hundred years; the most primitive
flintlocks. Others—including a ten-chambered Belgian
revolver—are modern. One of the most uncommon of
the lot is a double-barreled percussion cap pistol with
three triggers.

Two of the triggers are for the two barrels. The
third trigger releases the spring of a nine-inch bayonet
which snaps forward and turns the pistol into a rather
murderous knife.

An artillery colonel told me a few such weapons
were turned out in Great Britain, somewhere around
1826, with a view to their use by army officers, but
that the War Office frowned on them and no more
were made.

I have talked overlong about these weapons and armor-pieces of mine and without describing a tithe of them. At best the theme is of interest only to folk with the same juvenile passion for collecting them.

I have spoken of the arch which turns the living room and the music room into one L-shaped apartment. As its inner edge there is a stand whereon is an antique copper bowl inlaid with silver, shallow and perhaps thirty inches across. We bought it in the rather far past at a bazaar in the native city, at Algiers. Because we paid for it in American gold coins we could afford to buy it, after haggling the saddle-colored merchant down to a possible price.

From the earliest blooms of spring the bowl is heaped high with beauty. In early May, with a miniature forest of dogwood. Next with numberless glowing Florentine iris. Then with perhaps a hundred deep crimson June roses over which the afternoon sun streams in a blinding ruby light.

After that it is piled high with the roses and gladioli and dahlias of late summer. Then with a forest of gaudy October leaves. Last of all, in autumn, with long-stemmed fluffy giant chrysanthemums from the greenhouse. In winter, with a clump of holly leaves and holly berries.

Each season offers its timely tribute to the bowl.

Our friends who know Sunnybank turn first of all to the silver-and-copper bowl, when they come through the Dutch half-doors into the living room. A governor of New Jersey said:

"We can tell what season it is, just by one look at the Bowl."

The same light which glorifies the Bowl shines like a halo on the head and face of Honthorst's "Christ" just behind it, and on the portraits of the Mistress and of my father beyond the Steinway concert piano and the framed parchment pages of fifteenth century chorals.

The big piano fills the wall space between two of the music room's long French windows. It was under this piano that Sunnybank Lad had his "cave" for so many years. The windows open on the vine-hung veranda. When the Mistress begins to play, a dozen or more birds fly from all directions and perch among the veranda vines.

A catbird or two. Most of the others are song sparrows. The music seems to draw them thither. Sometimes they sit silent. But at the very first notes of a few things she plays, there is a chorus of accompaniment. The song sparrows, I think, are the only singers at these times.

The Spinning Song from Wagner's *Flying Dutchman* has some quality which sets them to singing at the top of their lungs, in ecstasy. So has a Chopin Etude in F major. Never in the spring or early summer does the Mistress play either of these without a multiple birdsong obbligato.

Years ago we had a pale gold "roller" canary, Bambino by name. His cage hung in the dining room. When he sang—which was throughout most of the daylight hours—two song sparrows always perched just outside the open windows and caroled with him. It was a shrilly sweet trio. Sometimes a catbird would turn it into a quartet.

At midnight, some seasons back, a nightingale in Beatrice Harrison's English garden was lured unwittingly to sing its glugging chant into a microphone. Short waves bore the golden bubblings to America. They reached Sunnybank before sunset, filling house and veranda with a melody unknown in this country. Every song sparrow, every catbird, every oriole, within earshot, sang in ecstasy. Sunnybank songbirds and a Surrey nightingale three thousand miles away were swelling the same mad chorus. . . . Yet folk scoff at miracles!

The music room's polished brown floor is three-quarters covered by an enormous snowy polar bear skin, on which the dogs are forbidden to lie. Similar polar bear skins and the pelts of leopards and brown bears and of tigers strew the living room's polished floors. From its walls glare down trophy heads.

Back in 1910 we engaged white maids, predecessors of our present black Martinique servants who have been with us for more than twenty-three years and who speak no language but French.

The housemaid came into the music and living rooms to dust, on the first morning of her stay with us. At breakfast time she sought out the Mistress and said:

"If white bears and brown bears and tigers and

leopards and wolves and suchlike critters roam so close to Sunnybank House that they can be shot and skinned, I think we maids better move back to town. You see, madam, we ain't used to such rough pets."

But we were talking about Sunnybank's downstairs rooms, not of timorous hirelings.

So much for the *downstairs* rooms. I won't drag you up the first flight of stairs; not even to the Mistress's shell-pink bedroom, twenty-six by thirty-two feet in area, with its six windows framed in wistaria; nor to the smaller and dainty "Violet Bedroom"—a guest chamber—just beyond it; nor to the rambling line of rooms on the floor above and to the crowded and wasp-haunted attic atop the house. Nor to the several big bathrooms. Though bathrooms are a fad of ours.

When we were children a half-century ago both of us lived in largish old houses occupied by largish old families. There, a single bathroom served the whole household. We were grateful for even that one bathroom; both of us remembering our sense of godless luxury when it was installed.

Going back for a moment to the Mistress's room for the sake of an odd happening there: At the north end of the room stands an old (not antique) wooden mantel-shelf, above the fireplace. It was nailed or otherwise fastened there when the house was built. It extends perhaps eighteen inches from its shelf down to where it ends at the top of the fireplace tiling.

One morning in 1932 the Mistress chanced to see a tiny green triangle tip protruding from the bottom of the mantel and outlined sharply against the tiles beneath. She pointed it out to me. We went to investigate. It had not been there an hour earlier.

The Mistress drew it down from its hiding place. It was the corner of a faded green card. A card bearing in dark red letters this inscription:

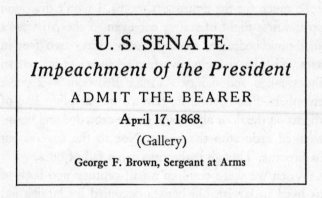

U. S. SENATE.
Impeachment of the President
ADMIT THE BEARER
April 17, 1868.
(Gallery)
George F. Brown, Sergeant at Arms

In 1868—sixty-four years before the Mistress saw the protruding green triangle—some statesman friend of my father's must have sent him this admittance ticket to the impeachment proceedings instituted against President Andrew Johnson.

I suppose the card had been put on the mantel top, soon after the post brought it to Sunnybank. Thence it had fallen through the narrow crack between the mantel and the wall behind it.

Bit by bit for more than six decades it had continued its downward progress, a fraction of an inch a year, jarred imperceptibly farther on its descent by every slam of a door, by every heavy footstep, by the driving of every picture nail.

It is back at its starting place now, atop the mantel and in a glass-fronted frame too thick to permit another vanishing through the half-invisible crack. It fell into our hands sixty-four years too late for us to accept its invitation.

As I said, the Mistress discovered it. And in 1868 the Mistress's grandfather, United States Senator John P. Stockton of New Jersey, was credited, more than any other member of the Senate, with having blocked the impeachment of Johnson. Which is a farfetched coincidence, if you like. To us it is mildly interesting.

A last word about Sunnybank's ground floor rooms:

There is one of these for which I have a queer fondness; though I don't go into it more than five times a year and then only to forage for a midnight feast. Yet in the few changes or projected changes in the house's interior I have refused stanchly to let it be abolished or altered.

It is a one-story tin-roofed storeroom, just off the kitchen wing. It is unfurnished except for its highrising shelves laden with tinned food and such things and for a barrel or two and for a single stiff old chair. It is at my wish that the rickety chair has been left there for these many decades.

When I was five years old and on for the next year or so, there was a thrill for me in that bare little storeroom. On rainy nights—when I had had my supper and the grown-ups were dressing for dinner—I used to sneak out there, carrying under my arm my adored white-and-black kitten, Antipathy; and the next year her fluffy child and successor, Deleterious.

(I thought the words, "antipathy" and "deleterious," by far the most exquisitely musical in all the language, even though I had not the slightest idea what either of them meant. So I bestowed them on my two kittens.)

With Antipathy snuggled warmly in my lap I would sit for half an hour in the dark storeroom; having a splendid time. The door to the adjoining laundry was open. So was the door from the laundry to the kitchen. The soft kitchen light crept faintly through to me. So did the much less soft voices of the maids preparing dinner. So did the heavenly blend of cooking smells.

The rain tattooed down on the tin roof with a most engaging sound. I was warm and cozy and hidden, and safe from the storm. The drowsy charm of it still is fresh with me.

But during those stolen half-hours—before I was retrieved and imbedded by my nurse—was I just a grubby small boy sitting in the dark on a stiff chair in an unwinsome cubbyhole of a storeroom and with a cat named Antipathy purring in my lap?

I was not.

I was the Ancient Mariner—my mother used to read that grisly classic aloud to me, often, at my stark pleading—who in some manner unauthorized by Coleridge had made his way to a rain-swept island.

There I had overcome the savages; who presently

showed good taste by choosing me as their king. Returning to my hut at nightfall, with a leopard I had caught and tamed during the day's rambles, I was sitting at rest on a pile of skins, listening to the tropical rain hammer of the thatched roof. My tamed leopard crouched across my knees. In the cooking cave, just beyond, my loving subjects were preparing a banquet for me.

To this day the somnolent patter of rain on a tin roof brings back to me the whole babyish drama and its setting.

Yes, it's silly of me not to let the storeroom enlarge the laundry by the ripping out of a wall; or to rip out the wall on the opposite side and thus give me needed extra space in my downstairs study. I know that. But—

It is such an endlessly dreary stretch of years since last I tamed a leopard or was elected king of a mythical island tribe! I like to keep the storeroom in its former state, as a monument to those brave days of my leopard-training kingship. What harm does it do?

CHAPTER FOUR

Chips, the Disreputable

SHE was going to be a stable dog. That was understood very clearly. She was to be fed at the stables and to have a shakedown bed behind the stalls. Her life duty was to be the wholesale wiping out of all the rats from the barns and from around the kennel yards. She was to earn her keep in that way.

For once, Sunnybank was to have a dog whose mission was grim utility alone. We did not expect to see much of her, except perhaps sometimes around the various outbuildings where she should be busily plying her trade of rat slaying.

We bought her.

Less than a week thereafter she was spending her nights on an old shooting coat of mine in a corner of my study. And always she lay at the Mistress's feet in the dining room at mealtimes. Moreover, a full year dragged by before she deigned to kill a single rat.

What I have just told you gives a better blueprint of Chips's character and of her absurd personality than ten thousand words of my labored description could supply.

She is a disreputable little Irish terrier, with all the queer charm and none of the stanchness of that splendid breed. But she is a right engaging little brute. Somehow she has wriggled her way into the hearts of all of us.

If you crave to read only of a professionally loyal dog, avid to risk life for its master—if you yearn for a sterling canine life-story capped by an infinitely pathetic death scene—then I am afraid this true yarn of mine won't make any kind of a hit with you.

Chips could no more fit into such a rôle than Charlie Chaplin could play Hamlet. And perhaps I lack the skill to explain at all convincingly how she won her way into a household which had planned in advance a life of drab usefulness for her.

The first thing that drew her to us was her name. And that name was given to her some eighteen months before she was born—a year and half before ever we planned to buy a stable dog.

I wrote a series of stories for the *Ladies' Home Journal*. The tales revolved about a heartless, winsome, harum-scarum pup named "Chips." I chose the name because it seemed in keeping with the fictional dog's nature.

(The stories appeared later in book form under the title, *A Dog Named Chips*.)

My old friend, Robert L. Dickey—"Bob" Dickey—illustrated the magazine tales. With his wonted uncanny cleverness he got inside the character of the dog

I portrayed. As a result, the pictures he drew embodied Chips to the life; and they gave a stark reality to the fictional terrier.

It was more than a year later that we had a visitation of rats at Sunnybank. Our vet told us we could get rid of them in a trice if only we would buy an Irish terrier. Such dogs, he said, were the natural enemy of the rat. A single Irish terrier would raven through the stables and kennels; and rout out and slay every rat that showed its whiskers aboveground.

More: such an Irish terrier would dig deep into the warrens and burrows; and would slaughter such rats as had not the sportmanship to face it in the open. The few rats that might escape the massacre would become so disheartened and panic-smitten that they would leave Sunnybank in a body.

Of course I was mildly sorry for the poor doomed things. But, after all, they were dirty pests. Their universal destruction would be a boon to us.

So the Mistress and I drove over to the Old Mill Kennels, a few miles from here, to buy the raticidal terrier. Before we went, we decided we wanted no house dogs but our collies. The newcomer must be kept in its place. And that place was to be the outbuildings. No cosseting; no chumship. The dog was to be a mere killing machine and was to have no point of contact with the house or with its occupants.

Well, we went through the Old Mill Kennels, studying one fine Irish terrier after another. All of them seemed good. But somehow none of them seemed to me just what I wanted for my purpose.

Perhaps because I had memories of a brace of glorious Irish terriers of more than a quarter century agone—Mickey Free and his wise little son, Paddy—that were hard to erase from my thoughts. Mickey and Paddy had been loved chums of mine in those far-off days before I waxed old.

As I happened to pass through the kennel office I stopped short. In the middle of the floor a five-month female Irish terrier was romping with a leash, to which she was doing direful things.

And the romping puppy was—*Chips*.

She was the perfect counterpart, in looks, in expression, in demeanor, of the dog in my stories; the raffish "Chips" which Bob Dickey's inspired pencil had made so real and so unmistakable.

She might well have posed for those Dickey drawings; though she had not been born when they were drawn or when my canine book heroine was named.

On a hunch I bought her, then and there.

I saw she was not of as good type as were most of her kennel mates. Indeed, she was of only tolerable type, from a show standpoint. But she was—she was *Chips!*

Her owner had named her "Mary"—of all things! —but I remedied that quickly enough by registering her with the American Kennel Club as "Sunnybank Chips," and by teaching her the new name.

Never had she been in a car. But we started home with her; the Mistress driving and I holding the puppy in my lap. On our way, ten minutes later, we stopped at the post office. A friend came forward to speak to us.

As he laid his hand on the car door, Chips went into action. Hitherto she had sat high and proudly, enjoying her first motor ride. Now, at the alien touch on the door of the car—HER car—she flew at the astonished man like a small red whirlwind.

Raging, snarling, foaming at the jaws, she made every possible effort to get at his throat. Nor would she stop her ungodly uproar until he departed. Then, as if she felt the car was safe once more, she snuggled down into my lap.

As we drove into the garage at Sunnybank, a few minutes afterward, my English superintendent, Robert Friend, came to the coupé door for a look at the future killer of rats.

Again the puppy flew into a murderous fury at the man who dared open the door of her sacred car—it had been hers, man and boy, for nearly twenty minutes in all—and she sprang ragingly at him.

Mind you, she was only five months old; and it was her very first experience as a car dog. But she was on the job. No rabid she-wolf could have been more terrible in guarding its lair.

I picked her up and set her on the ground outside. Instantly, she ceased to be a car-demon and became a frisky and friendly and tumultuous puppy; fond of everyone and of everything.

This was the start.

From that day until now, she has been mildness itself toward all mankind, except when she is in a motor car. At such times her spear has known no brother. She is gracious to the Mistress and myself when we go driving. But no outsider can come within ten feet of the machine, unchallenged by her.

Worse: presently her car-guarding instinct led her to adopt all the automobiles in the world as her own. Eagerly she clambered into every machine that came to Sunnybank; if only its door was open. Once there, she prepared to defend the vehicle against all humanity.

Last year, friends of ours drove out here from Tuxedo for lunch. When they were ready to go home, they sent for their limousine. It did not come up from the garage. But their chauffeur did. The man's face was purple with wrath. He was fondling a badly bitten thumb and forefinger.

"I went around the kennels to have a look at the Sunnybank collies I'd read about," he explained ruefully. "When I got back to the car a little red dog had hopped up onto the front seat. I tried to coax her out. (She was shedding her coat and she'd got a million loose red hairs smeared all over the cushions.) But she went for me like she was crazy. This is what she done to me. She won't let me get into the car, nohow. Somebody that likes bites better'n I do has got to lift her out of there before we can start."

But I am getting a year or two or three years ahead of our story.

I told you we bought Chips as a rat-killer. After she had had time to get used to her new home—which was very little time indeed—I instituted the first *battue*—or "rattue," as the Mistress called it.

The Mistress herself would not stay to watch the carnage. She doesn't like such things.

But Robert Friend and the other men and I turned Chips loose in a big barnyard where rats had grown so bold as to run to and fro without fear. It was dog feeding time. Five rats scuttled across the enclosure. We watched for the ferocious devastation. There was none.

Chips eyed the scurrying rodents as you or I might watch some passing ant or a cockroach. She was not even mildly interested.

The rats, too, seemed to understand they had nothing to fear from the perky little terrier. One or two of them passed fearlessly within snapping distance of her funny little inefficient jaws. She let them go.

There was something wrong, somewhere, in the vet's forecast of wholesale annihilation. So I telephoned him.

"She's only just a baby, yet," he answered my complaint of Chips's cold non-interest in the rats. "Only five months old, you say? Give her time. She's due to be a holy terror with them in another few months. Maybe sooner."

So we gave her time. And she took plenty of it. She used those days of grace in fortifying her position with us; strutting into the house ahead of us and making herself comically at home there; investigating every nook and corner of it. She was one of those rare pups which don't need to be housebroken.

Though all of our abode seemed to meet with her cold approval, she chose my study as her home. Pulling from a peg my outworn tweed shooting coat —Poole, of Savile Row, London, built it for me; and may he forgive the desecration!—she spread it neatly on the floor in one corner and lay down to sleep on it. Thenceforth, and today, that has been her bed.

Why did we tolerate such proceedings? Why did we let her swagger into the dining room and nestle at the Mistress's feet during meals? Why did we let her assume the rôle of pampered housedog, when she belonged in the stables; we who know dogs and who know how they should be handled and kept in their place? The best answer I can give to these rhetorical questions is:

"I'm blest if I know!"

A wiser reply would be:

"She is Chips."

Often I have wondered at our weakness in letting her promote herself at once to housedogship. It is not in the very least like either the Mistress or myself. But when Personality clashes with Principles, mere Principles are prone to go to the wall.

Then came her meeting with our other dogs. They were collies. Collies do not bully or abuse a small dog. At least, that has been my lifelong experience with them. They fight like tigers, if need be. But only

with other large dogs. So I had no fear that any of
them would maltreat the swanky little newcomer.
They did not.

Chips seemed to realize this. For she imposed
frightfully on them. For instance, she would jump
up and wrest a bone from between the jaws of some
majestic collie; and carry it off, unscathed. She would
tease and pester the big dogs to the top of her bent.
They endured it; as you might endure the teasing
of a baby.

But on a day she made the error of shoving her
auburn muzzle into the feed dish from which huge
Sunnybank Victrix had just begun to eat her dinner.
Victrix was as gentle as she was big. But nothing on
The Place could impose upon her. She put one forepaw firmly on Chips's back and proceeded to roll
the terrier puppy over and over on the ground.

Victrix did not nip her, nor so much as growl. Nor
did the gentle pushes of her forepaw bruise her victim.
But she did her job thoroughly and with much sad
dignity.

And Chips? Did the punished youngster fight gallantly back at the collie? She did not.

Wiggling impotently, with her paws tucked under
her and with her eyes rolling as fast as her slim body,
she made no effort to retaliate. Instead, her screeches
of craven terror assailed high heaven. Seldom have I
seen an instance of cowardice more pitiable.

After that, Chips let the collies alone when they
were eating; and she went far more gingerly in her
teasing of them at any time.

Though she would not hunt rats, she developed a mania for chasing hornets. When one of the sinister insects happened to fly across the veranda, she was after it in mad haste; leaping high and snapping at the elusive creature. Life's greatest ambition, just then, with Chips, was to catch a hornet.

She caught one.

I saw her leap up, snapping. Her funny jaws found their goal. Then she shrieked in deafening anguish. And she came bounding across the veranda to where I sat. Fleeing to me for refuge she sprang into my lap— the vengeful hornet arriving there almost as soon as she did.

The incident taught her that it was pleasant to sit in my lap—a morbid preference, at best; with few to compete with her for the coveted place. After that she was forever jumping up into my lap, sitting there in state as she did in a car.

The pleasure was all hers. For she was growing larger and bonier. There are more comfortable things for the sittee than to have a dog of many angles sit thus.

She varied her procedure, on this reluctant human perch. Sometimes she would sit aloft, looking like Rameses II. Again she would cuddle down to sleep. Then, hearing some dog bark in the distance, she would give a mighty leap into space, to find out what the barking was about.

And she would use my tortured stomach as a "take off" for the jump. Again, the pleasure was all hers.

For me, the whole proceeding had not one redeeming trait; and I put a stop to it. I am a collie man. I don't care for lap dogs. Especially when they are all sharp angles and when they brace their hind feet against my meridian in springing into space.

Chips grew older. Still, rats meant less than nothing in her glad life, though she slew four of the five stable cats in fast succession. I had bought her for a ratter. Not a catter. Again I consulted the vet who had lured me into buying her. He assured me:

"It's because she hasn't had any experience, yet, in killing rats. Let her get her teeth into one of them, just once;—and heaven help the rest of the rat tribe at Sunnybank! If a rat was 'winged' now, and she could get at it—"

That was enough. I went out at feeding time with a target rifle. A big rat scrambled across the barnyard, just in front of Chips. I wounded him in the leg. He began circling around Chips like a patent toy. She did not so much as honor his circular hobblings with a glance.

But Sandy—Sunnybank Sandstorm—swooped down upon the injured rodent and broke its back. Instantly, Chips saw the rat was a toy of sorts. She snatched it from Sandy's unwilling jaws, and galloped out of sight with it.

Now this was better. She was having her first experience in grabbing a rat. It would arouse in her the dormant blood lust—the instinct to slay and slay and slay; until not one live rat should be left within a mile of Sunnybank.

Thirty seconds later, she came cantering back to me, and leered up into my face. The rat had vanished. (That evening after dark, when I sat down on the veranda, I found the missing and messy rodent. Chips had deposited it on the seat of my favorite porch chair. I was wearing spotless new white flannels, too!)

For many a month thereafter, Chips would not pay the remotest attention to rats.

Then a litter of collie puppies was born. From the outset, Chips showed the keenest interest in these fluffy babies. By the hour she would stand, head on one side, stubby tail up, just outside their broodnest.

When they were six weeks old and were transferred to the big puppy-yard, Chips took up her vigil at the edge of the wired enclosure. All day she would watch the pups' clumsy gambols; and she would lick their faces when they strayed near enough to the wire.

Then Chips acquired the fear that the puppies were starving to death. This despite the fact that they were fatter than tubs of lard; and had much more food offered them than they could eat.

She began bringing unsavory bones to their yard —bones she had dug up—and trying to shove them through the wire meshes.

The pups scorned her generous gifts. So she went farther afield. Her latent ancestral instincts awoke, under this new stress. To the barnyard she ran. Thence, presently, she returned, bearing in pride a rat she had just killed—her first—and pushing its limp and gory body through the meshes.

On that day alone she killed and brought to the puppies seven large rats. True, the pups would not touch the grisly offerings. But Chips had learned at late last the joys of ratting.

Since then she has been a paragon at that thrilling sport. An inspired ratter. The rat population of Sunnybank has dwindled accordingly to a mere nothing.

Vastly proud of heart was Chips at the praise meted out to her for her new accomplishment. It went to her head. As you shall see.

Last autumn several guests were here one morning. To the back veranda we wandered, Chips strutting close beside us. She was strutting and swaggering more than usual, by reason of the attentions that had just been paid to her. Knowing her as I did, I was on the lookout for something. But not wholly for what happened.

Behind the rear veranda there are some seventy feet of greensward. Then, between the kennels and the lawn rises a high honeysuckle hedge. In the middle of the hedge is a great clump of honeysuckle; a veritable jungle of it.

As we stood on the porch, Chips moved in front of us. Her hackles were bristling. Her whole wiry body was tense and vibrant. Her lips were curled back. Her comedy face wore the look of a raging tiger. Deep in her throat she snarled.

Then she hurled herself forward like a flung spear. Across the patch of rear lawn she sped. High in air she arose. She plunged deep down into the jungle of honeysuckle vine.

Out of it she sprang again. Between her teeth was an enormous rat. She shook the rat, vehemently. Next she tossed its slain body above her head. She caught it, as it came down, with a rib-crushing grip.

She ended the scene by flinging the rat heavily to the earth, and standing victoriously with one forepaw planted on it.

My guests were deeply impressed by this dramatic bit of work. So was I. But I was not quite as deeply impressed as were they.

For, an hour earlier, I had made the round of the kennels, with Chips swanking along beside me. I had found in a trap an excessively dead rat. I had opened the trap and had picked the rat up by the tail and had tossed him into that smother of honeysuckle vine.

Twice again, the same day, for the benefit of later guests, Chips went through the same rat-slaying drama. Both times with the same defunct rat which she had carried back between-whiles to the same hiding place.

Do you wonder her crazy personality has won her a sleeping place in my study and a position of honor under the Mistress's chair in the dining room?

She is 100 per cent unworthy. But she is—Chips!

CHAPTER FIVE

Our "Garden from Everywhere"

My MOTHER's mother began our "Garden From Everywhere." She began it before Sunnybank House was half built. She didn't know she was laying the foundation for an exotic hodgepodge garden which was to endure all this time amid our more conventional blooms.

But she had strange power over every variety of plant. Whether she loved them or not, I don't know. But assuredly they loved her. They did things for her that they would do for no one else. All her life she had wrought with tree and vine and blossom and shrub. And she wanted her daughter's new home to be adorned by the best-liked of them.

My grandmother must have come logically by her hobby. For an ancestress of hers sailed to America from Devonshire in 1632, bringing along a handful of weeping willow twigs from her English home, Olney. These she replanted at her husband's Virginia plantation, which she named Olney in memory of her birthplace.

The willows throve finely in the New World soil. Thenceforth they and their offshoots were salient features of the plantation.

My grandmother cut a sheaf of the Olney willow twigs and brought them to Sunnybank. She planted them in a line at our lake edge, at the foot of the orchard. Today they are huge and gnarled and aged. But they are as vigorous as ever and they form a green cataract between orchard and lake.

At Olney, in Virginia, was an ancient woodbine, which battled with the wistaria for mastery on the plantation's dead trees. Family tradition—true or not—said both vines had been raised from slips grown at the English Olney. When my grandparents moved to Richmond, during my mother's early childhood, they brought along slips of both the wistaria and the woodbine. Soon the house they had bought, on Leigh Street, was half-buried in their foliage.

Slips of each were carried by my grandmother to Sunnybank and were planted here. Here they live now. The woodbine forms ropes of dark green— aflame in October—between two trees. It rises in a fat pyramid over a third tree, a cedar. It strangled the cedar to death long ago. But it increased tenfold its victim's foliage effects.

By the way, that cedar-emeritus rates a disciplinary visit from a Tenement House Commission. I am quite certain it contains an illegally large number of families. It is honeycombed from top to bottom and all the way across with nests of every variety of bird from chipping sparrow to blue jay. Nor do the crowded families get on any too well with one another.

The imported wistaria was planted by my grandmother along the edge of the new-built veranda. Its main stem had grown to more than thirty-seven inches in circumference, some ten years ago. Then one of its own suckers twined around it—a sucker more thick than my own ample wrist—and killed it. But it had had plenty of children to take its place.

The house and the arbors are rife with it. In May there is a half acre of lavender blur where the hanging blooms blot out everything behind them. On moon-drenched spring nights, the soft air is heavy with the fragrance. Those are nights when our gray deep veranda becomes fairyland and when we, who sit there, drop our voices unconsciously as one does in entering a church.

At every season of the year—except during the dead months—the veranda is our evening resort. On it and from it one sees beauty which almost hurts.

From the early spring nights when the air is thick with perfume and when it echoes to the trill of the lake-verge frogs—on through the solemn black nights of midsummer—and through to the time when nature dies—there is a nameless charm to the old porch; a charm that has gripped many others besides the Mistress and myself.

Also there are sporadic visits from mosquitoes.

Presently this rambling dissertation of mine will get to the actual Garden From Everywhere. But let

me strain your patience a little longer with a tale dealing indirectly with the woodbine and the wistaria
from the old Leigh Street house in Richmond.

I can remember when Leigh Street was stately and
gracious; when pleasant old families still lived there
where they had dwelt for generations. Then evil
times fell upon the street. The wide houses were deserted by their olden occupants. Negro boarding
houses crept in. My grandparents' erstwhile home
was taken over as a kind of Salvation Army shelter
or something akin to it.

My mother was visiting her brother in another part
of Richmond in the spring of 1921. She was more than
ninety years old and she was stone blind. My wife and
I stopped over for a day or so on our way north from
Florida. And my mother insisted on taking us to the old
Leigh Street house.

When we arrived there—and I had been forewarned
what it would be like—I threw a massive tip in to the
janitor to clear out and to keep the down-at-heel tenants
away from us. Sightless, but unerring as to her direction, my mother led the way into a rough-boarded
little first floor cubbyhole to the right of the front
door,—the whole first floor was a sorry place split up
into dirty cubicles. I guided her steps so she should not
come in contact with the impromptu walls. Pausing, she
said:

"This was our drawing room, when I was a girl.
It fills the whole side of the house, you see. Is it well
kept up, now?"

In one breath the Mistress and I assured her it was. We made the same vehement assurance when she pointed to a long-gone fireplace and to a massive non-existent stairway leading down into the room.

It was harder for us to keep our voices politely enthusiastic when she pointed out of a window to a ghastly dirt expanse strewn with muck and garbage.

"I'm so glad the people who live here keep the dear old garden as lovely as it used to be," she said. "Mother took such pains in laying it out and in tending it. I know how happy she would be to know it hasn't been changed. You'll see how all the paths with their box borders and flower beds verge toward that summerhouse in the center. In another month, the jasmine blossoms will cover every inch of it. In that jasmine summerhouse, back in eighteen-fifty-five, your father asked me to marry him."

No, it wasn't funny. It wasn't even pathetic. Her eager blank eyes were seeing the whole place far more accurately than were we. We saw only the squalor and filth and desolation of it. My mother saw it with the clearness of a hundred golden memories.

It was my mother, by the way, who had followed her own mother's footsteps in building up the idea of our Sunnybank Garden From Everywhere. For instance:

As she and I were wandering through the Medici garden in Florence, in 1893, we came upon a glory of deep purple Florentine iris; of a hue and variety neither of us had seen in America. We bribed the wizened little guide to give us three or four of its bulbs.

By some conjuring trick inherited from her mother, she coaxed these bulbs into remaining fresh—and unseen by customs folk—until we reached home.

Today there are hundreds of those deep purple iris at Sunnybank; all descended from the handful of bulbs we suborned the guide into selling us. They are georgeously handsome.

To a very few close friends of ours in recent years the Mistress and I have given a bulb or two. Wherefore the Medici iris is blossoming nowadays in divers places from Altadena, California, to Valley Stream, Long Island.

In England, as we walked through quaint old William Cowper's quaint old garden, my mother tipped the guide to let her break off a sprig of Cowper's famed southernwood. She nursed that sprig for months, as if it had been an ailing child. Then she planted it at Sunnybank. Three great bushes of it grow here now. When the sun beats down on them the pungent scent is like a whiff of old-fashioned smelling salts.

At Pompeii she picked a half dozen seed-pods of the sweet alyssum which fills the crevices of the walls and the cracked pavements. The seeds took right kindly to Sunnybank soil. Their bloom forms many yards of the path borders here.

It was so with rosemary snipped by permission from Anne Hathaway's garden at Shottery; with an ivy slip from the Black Prince's Well; with a rose cutting

from a Provence monastery graden; with an array of
other slips and seeds and bulbs from all over Europe;
with a cyclamen root I brought her from atop one of the
rocky Galilee hills in Palestine.

All of them lived, under her inspired nursing. All
of them lived and flourished when she transplanted
them at Sunnybank.

The Mistress and I have followed the pretty idea,
off and on, during our own foreign rambles:

Heather from the Blasted Heath where Macbeth
met the three witches. Strong ivy from a sprig the
verger picked for us from the Ivy-mantled Tower of
Gray's *Elegy*.

(You will seek long before you can get a cutting of
ivy from that church tower, today. The last time we
were at Stoke Pogis every vestige of the vine had been
ripped from its ancient abiding place on plea that it
was injuring the mortar and loosening the stones.)

A violet root the verger dug from alongside Gray's
tomb in the divine old churchyard has spread wide
and lustily and with numberless flowers since we
planted it here. So has a sprig of ice-vine our Majorca
guide picked for us from the wall of green that shrouded
the castle's towers.

On one of our lazy visits to the ruins of Kenilworth
Castle, the Mistress pointed out to me a mass of golden
wallflowers growing atop the tower which Cromwell
smashed. She said:

"I wish your mother could have seen those. She told
me she loved them better than any other flower."

The Kenilworth guide had been an actor in Benson's company in times when his aging voice was strong enough to fill a playhouse—in the years before he was forced to satisfy his powers of declamation by quoting pages of Shakespeare to idly bored tourists.

The oldster had struck up an acquaintance with the Mistress and myself during other visits. Now he said:

"Give me your address in the States, won't you?"

He scribbled it, while I wondered morosely whether he might be planning a series of begging letters to us.

A few months afterward we received from him an envelope containing a packet of seeds, and a card whereon he had written:

"Your mother's favorite flower. I had a boy climb the tower as soon as the blossoms went to seed, and get these for you."

The seeds grew well here. Today we have a border of golden wallflowers whose ancestors bloomed atop Kenilworth Castle. They are fit recruits to our Garden From Everywhere.

As a little chap, in Springfield, Massachusetts, I reveled in the wealth of wildflowers which carpeted the fields around the city in early May. Best of them all I liked the clumps of pale blue four-petaled blooms, perhaps three times the size of forget-me-nots.

The other children called them "Mayflowers." But grown-ups told me that was not correct and that the true Mayflower was the arbutus. The star-like pale blue blossoms, they told me, were "bluets," or "innocence."

I kept on calling them Mayflowers. I used to gather great bunches of them and take them to a girl who was younger than I, but who was my best-liked chum. True, by the time I got them to her home in my grubby fists, the once-dainty Mayflowers were in a state of advanced wiltedness. Yet she seemed pleased with the gift.

(Not that it has anything to do with this meandering yarn, but I went back to Massachusetts in 1901 and married her.)

Always these bluets or innocence or Mayflowers have been associated in my mind with the Massachusetts meadows. Never had I seen them elsewhere. A few years ago the Mistress and I were motoring through the Berkshires. At the road-edge outside a field the ground was covered with clumps of them.

They were on no man's land—or, rather, on the right of way—yet I wrought carfeully to dig up only three clumps and in spots where their absence would leave no gap.

Home to Sunnybank we brought them. The next spring they bloomed gaily and their scattered seeds had come up in several places. Their blossoming continued for a full six weeks.

I was proud of this acquisition to our Garden From Everywhere. So when I went on my yearly spring pilgrimage to Chester Jay Hunt's Mayfair Gardens at Little Falls to revel in his acres of impossibly splendid tulips and woodflowers, I bragged to him of my new importations. I told him the bluets grew nowhere but in New England.

For answer he stepped over a fence and across into an uncultivated field. Thence he brought back to me a double handful of my loved Mayflowers, roots and all.

I planted them at Sunnybank, but with little of my former thrill. I had traveled nearly two hundred miles for flowers which grow just as lushly within five miles of my own home. Still, imported or domestic, the bluets are beautiful. And they have thriven in our Garden From Everywhere.

I am glad to have these souvenirs of the Berkshires, a region of which the Mistress and I never tire; a region where roads are fine, yet where those roads are laid out so as to be as stimulating to the eye as to the speedometer.

The Massachusetts villages and small towns are as beautiful as the average New Jersey and southern New York village is ugly. And the hills have a benignity and a friendliness that make me think of the hills that gird Sunnybank.

A "life-plant" smuggled through from Bermuda also has grown lustily; though it and our Majorca ice-plant must be taken into the greenhouse in winter.

The life-plant is a non-spectacular weed with fat leaves. In Bermuda it sends up a high stalk in its center. From the stalk pink bulbs like capsules hang down. From the end of each capsule sprout a half dozen bright red pointed petals. But it is the fleshy leaves that give the plant its name.

I found a scatter of these leaves, last week—fallen from a plant carried illegally into this country and given to me. They were lying strewn on a shelf in the greenhouse. There they had lain for months. They were as fresh as if they had been picked an hour earlier.

From the edges of several of the leaves tiny roots bristled into the air, supporting tiny green plants of their own, already a half-inch high.

The stemless leaves, lying long on that bare shelf, not only had stayed freshly alive but had thrown forth vigorous little shoots from their serried edges.

I saw life-plants, first, clinging to crannies on walls along the snow-white Bermuda roads. Next I saw them, larger and in bloom, in the wondrous sunken garden behind the Castle Harbour Hotel, in Bermuda.

That several-acre sunken garden behind the Castle Harbour, by the way, is one of the three most beautiful sights of my pleasantly misspent long life. It is a thing of breathless exquisiteness. But as it is on the far side of the vast building from the bar and the swimming pool, I doubt if ten guests in a hundred have found it.

I said the sunken garden behind the Castle Harbour Hotel is to me one of a trio of perfect beauty spots. The second is the early morning vista down the main street of Stockbridge, Massachusetts, from the porch steps of the Red Lion Inn.

(That historic inn, by the way, serves food which is one of life's compensations. It seems like a waste of gracious gifts for its porch steps to be the starting point for so perfect a view.)

The third of the trio of visions is the sunset outlook across the lake from our Sunnybank veranda.

Justice tells me of a fourth view in my collection of

beauty pictures. The view of Havana Harbor at sunrise.

For years that scene throbbed in my myriad travel recollections. But, last time I sailed into the harbor at dawn a tepid rain was sluicing down in pailfuls. Everything was gray and sloppy and glum. So—humanlike—nowadays I remember it that way.

But there is a place which all-but fills the vacant niche left by the knockdown of the Havana picture. It is in Stockbridge, at the far end of the elm-arched main street from the Red Lion. An easy walk from the inn, even for a motor tourist.

It is reached through the main expanse of Stockbridge's lovely cemetery—ancient Acre of God where sleep the town's pioneers and Cyrus Field and Joseph Choate and David Dudley Field and many another great American—and where without a carven word of explanation the effigy of a setter dog lies at the foot of one grave.

At the farthest side from the highroad the cemetery seems to end in a fifteen-foot evergreen hedge, impenetrable, dense as a wall.

But in the center of the hedge is a narrow gap—almost imperceptible from a short distance—with a little iron gate swinging ajar. Go through this hidden gate, preferably at sunset in May, and you come upon sheer beauty.

It is a space, high-walled on every side by the dark green hedge—an enclosure perhaps two hundred feet square—the private burial place of the Sedgwicks.

At the outer edges of the oval is a circle of tall pine trees, white lilacs, climbing roses, black-green cedars; sentinels standing guard over ever-narrowing circles of white tombstones in whose center are two snowy monuments.

The lush grass is thick with little white flowers and there are low shrubs and many different kinds of blossoms. Always on such afternoons I have heard the songs of myriad birds that troop thither at sunset.

There is a still charm about this hidden plot akin to that of the English Cemetery at Rome—the cemetery whereof Shelley sighed that it was enough to make one in love with death.

In my wanderings through the Sedgwick burial lot I have come upon two graves whose stones puzzle me. I shall never know the answer. Yet I continue to puzzle.

One is a small rustic cross—presumably of metal, and carved and colored to look like rough wood— with the words "Our Helen" on a ribbon-like adornment over the crossbar.

At the foot of the grave sits an effigy, of the same material, of a short-haired dog built like a heavier Irish terrier. The thick collar around his throat bears the name "GRIP."

Ever his carven face is turned in worshipful alertness toward the name on the cross. I wish I might know the story.

(Stockbridge's, by the way, is the only quasi-modern cemetery in which I have seen the effigies of two dogs at the foot of graves.)

The second stone in the Sedgwick lot which seems

to have a story behind it is a time-stained slab erected to "Elizabeth Freeman, known by the name of MAUM-BET. Her supposed age was 85 years. She was born a slave and remained a slave for nearly thirty years. . . . Died 1829. . . . She never violated a trust nor failed to perform a duty. . . . Good Mother, Farewell."

A final handful of flowers from our Garden From Everywhere:

Some ten hours north by train from San Francisco is a California that makes no loud bid for tourists; a California that held an unforgettable charm for us. Wide and sheep-strewn valleys dotted by bright little towns and bounded on either side by giant mountain walls.

To the north, Mount Shasta shuts off the vista with what looks like a gargantuan mound of vanilla ice cream. To westward rises another ice-cream giant, Mount Lassen, our only non-extinct volcano, with vapor hanging always above its crest of eternal snow.

The foothills are splashed with acres of living gold —acres of California poppies. We were told these might not do well in the East. But we took a chance at gathering seeds and roots.

Some of the seeds have sprouted here at Sunnybank, though only a few of them. The California poppy has done less well for us than has almost any other of our importations. But enough of the blooms come out every summer to repay our bother in bringing their seeds across the continent, and to add flecks of pale gold to our Garden From Everywhere.

From hundreds of miles farther south in California

we brought home to Sunnybank slips of fiery red geraniums from the Mission of San Juan Capistrano and rose cuttings from the Santa Barbara Mission.

These were gifts. Not thefts. They have done wondrously well here.

Rather near the edge of the Mohave Desert begins a highroad which stretches like a sword for twenty-eight miles to Bakersfield. The road might well have been laid out by a twenty-eight-mile wooden ruler. For there are no curves nor bends in it. Never have I seen another road of its kind.

As we came down into it from the mountains, on the way from Los Angeles, the nearer foothills on either side looked as if some crazy impressionist painter had had a brainstorm among them. There were quarter-mile splotches of blue, of red, of poisonous yellow, at close intervals along the brown slopes —lupin and wild mustard and other vivid blooms.

More as a memento of the scene than for any better reason, we brought back with us some of the most flaring of the lupin. It has done well during its years of exile here in our Garden From Everywhere.

As for the wild mustard which we transplanted from the California hillsides, it has done far too well. It is a pest. That was one of our several blunders in the upbuilding of our garden.

Still, even the wild mustard brings back memories. And memories frrom the happiest element of our Garden From Everywhere. Each plant and flower in it brings us lasting pictures of their birthplaces.

The picture may be of a dreaming old Florentine

garden or of the grounds of a monastery in southern France or of a Warwickshire lane or of a Highland moor or of Greek ruins or of a multi-hued California mountainside. It may be typified by a glory of Provence roses or by a rank weed.

But always it *is* a picture, always a fragrant memory.

On the Acropolis at Athens I saw curlingly serrated long leaves radiating from a central stem and lying close to the ground. I asked my dragoman, Papadapoulos (you can say the name quite easily if you have a slight impediment in your speech), what the graceful plant might be.

He told me it was acanthus. I vowed to carry a root of it to Sunnybank. It was deemed a weed, in Greece, where it grew in every field. But the classics are full of its praise. Poets from Homer to Tennyson spoke favorably of it. And it was used in stone to adorn the capitals of temple columns and all that kind of thing. It was a grand addition to my garden. I brought it home.

It grew luxuriantly, here; not only in summer, but riding out the iciest winters and coming up afresh in early spring. On the very first year it put forth golden blossoms, wide and with petals like aureate hair.

Very showy it was, in its own way. But already we had thousands of its kind everywhere in our North Jersey fields.

My tenderly cherished Greek acanthus was a common dandelion!

* *

CHAPTER SIX

Our Sunnybank Bird Chums

I TOSSED a scrap of dry toast from our breakfast table in a vine-hid corner of the Sunnybank veranda. The morsel fell on the edge of the lawn just beyond the driveway. By the time it touched ground, a chipping sparrow pounced on it.

A song sparrow fluttered from a nest in the wistaria and drove away the tiny chipping sparrow. As the victor was pecking at the captured toast, he caught the attention of a robin that was cruising the lawn for worms.

The robin hopped over with an idea of varying his fare with vegetable diet. At his onset, the song sparrow fled. In leisurely relish the robin sampled the toast. But he pecked only once.

There was a challenging squawk. A flash of gray-ish blue dropped from a nest in a cedar tree, straight downward at the robin and his meal. Sulkily the robin retreated; and a bristling blue jay stooped greedily above the toast.

Before the jay could do more than glance at his plunder, a hole in the gray trunk of a hickory tree was blocked by a splash of fiery scarlet. In the tree tunnel a pair of red-headed woodpeckers were rearing their slate-hued fledglings. True pirate of his little world, the woodpecker launched himself at the toast. Yelling his wrongs to high heaven, the jay flew back into the cedar. Only to defend its own brood will a jay dare to withstand the redhead's charge.

The woodpecker came to earth alongside the toast. Insolently he put one claw on it. Still more insolently he looked up at the Mistress and myself, as we sat at the breakfast table not ten feet from him. That moment of delay cost him the food he had captured.

For there was a winnowing of wings from over the top of the house; and four of the snowy stable pigeons settled down on the lawn. Size and numbers were against the red-head freebooter. As two of the pigeons hurried with outthrust necks toward the toast, the woodpecker flew back in noisy wrath to the tree-hole.

The foremost pigeon was reaching for the oft-disputed trophy, when the kitchen cat loafed around the corner of the veranda. The cat crouched for a spring—more from habit than hunger, I think—as she came in view of the pigeons. But the gesture told a sinister ancestral story to the four white birds.

With much beating of the air, they rose from their untasted feast. The cat minced lazily forward. Before her sniffing nostrils could classify the food, our big collie, Sandy, had leaped from his resting place on the veranda floor, beside my chair; and had cleared the porch edge at a bound.

Merrily he dashed at the cat—with which, as a rule, he was on very comfortable terms. He craved only the oft-repeated fun of chasing her under the porch. He would not have hurt her; and she must have known it.

Yet she swelled her tail to three times its wonted size, scratched her tormentor's nose with unnecessary virulence; and fled spitting and yowling toward the refuge of the kitchen.

Sandy lounged forward to see what titbit had attracted her. He smelt scornfully at it; and returned to his place beside my chair. Sandy doesn't care for dry toast.

It was then that the chipping sparrow slipped unobtrusively back to the deserted battlefield. He speared the toast, and flew away with his burden to the safety of his invisible nest.

In less than sixty seconds, the world-old chain of conflict between strong and weak, aggressor and meek, had been forged and reforged, for our benefit. Yes, and in that same brief time the meek had inherited the earth—or at least the toast.

This incident was not especially worth telling, perhaps; unless to show the progressive forms of bullying in bird-and-beast life. But I chanced to speak of it to a friend. His sole reaction was of wonder that the several birds of several kinds should carry on their activities undisturbed by the presence of two humans only a few feet away.

It was his comment that made me realize for the first time how completely our Sunnybank birds seem to have admitted us into their daily lives; and how they accept the knowledge that they have nothing to fear from us.

I think they rather like us. Assuredly they have not the faintest respect for us. For, again and again, chipping sparrows or song sparrows or wrens hop to our very feet as we are at breakfast or at lunch in our veranda corner. If they find no crumbs strewn there for them, they stand and scold us shrilly until they are fed; or even hop up onto the table to do their own foraging.

Perhaps it is because they like to live close to their work, that no fewer than eleven birds couples built their nests in the veranda vines last spring. Perhaps it is because no guns are fired on our land and because the kitchen cat is kept from the vines and the trees, that the bird colonies choose our house and the nearer portions of the grounds for a summer resort.

Or perhaps it is because crumbs have been scattered for them and suet has been hung all winter in the trees, for more than three-quarters of a century.

My parents began to keep open house for the birds when, as young people, they built Sunnybank; many years before I was born. The custom has not been allowed to lapse. The Place has remained an all-year restaurant for generation after generation of its feathered guests.

A political economy professor complained to me once, in all seriousness:

"But don't you see you're pauperizing the birds by doing that? You are unfitting them to be anything but a charge on the community."

Perhaps we are. Who knows? And who cares? They are our good little friends; and we get endless entertainment from them.

Ornithological experts feel a still greater contempt for us than did the political economist. This because the Mistress and I have not the remotest technical knowledge of our bird chums. Neither of us knows an orchard oriole from a Baltimore oriole; nor a wood thrush from a Wilson thrush; nor one kind of a vireo from another. Indeed, it was only a short while ago that we learned a snowbird's real name is "junco."

We do not want to gain any book lore whatever, about our queer little bird people. We are well content with the wholly useless, but wholly delightful, inexact knowledge we have of them. They are our friends. They amuse us. And we feed them in return. We let it go at that.

More and more every year the Linnæan Society and the Audubon groups are making popular study of birds. But it is a form of study which somehow fails to enthuse us, here at Sunnybank.

If people enjoy that kind of thing, then in all likelihood that is the kind of thing they enjoy. But, to me, there would be just as much jolly human interest in classifying typhoid germs or B-Coli bacilli, as to set one's self to mastering the technicalities of bird names and species and differentia and the like.

We have one special stretch of fenced hillside woodland at Sunnybank, sloping down to the lake. It is a thick oak grove, full of mystic green shadows and golden glints; an elfin wood. It is a haven for pheasant and partridge in winter; and a loved abiding place for thrushes in spring and summer.

At sunset or at early dusk or at dawn its holy silences are athrob with thrush-songs. The Mistress and I go there at such times to listen; wordless, spellbound. To a hidden pool, near the lake-verge, one thrush after another comes to bathe; thence to fly to the oak-tops to swell the morning-or-evening chorus of a hundred voices. There is something indescribably exquisite in these concerts and in the time and the place.

One sunset we took several bird-expert guests down there, to revel with us in the unearthly music. By instinct and by custom, our own voices dropped to whispers as we entered the zone of enchantment.

But our better-versed guests shattered the spell by fairly shouting in exhultation and competition the book names of the various species of thrush whose notes they were able to classify. Loudest of all did they acclaim the presence of a flute-songed hermit thrush in a far reach of the wood.

For only a moment or two did their clamor endure. After that there was nothing to clamor about. For the birds lapsed into shocked silence at the uproar; and there were no further songs to dissect.

The Mistress and I had heard only the heaven-sent glory of it all. Our wise friends had shocked that glory into sick stillness by tabulating it.

Thanks; if it is all the same to the world at large—of if it is not—she and I will continue to look and listen from our hearts; not from an ornithological book. The Linnæans can go their way, if only they will let us go ours. I think we are the winners, not they.

Yet I do many of these experts a wrong in lumping them as mere scientific classifiers of birds. Some, to my knowledge, couple their technical lore with a real and deep love for their theme. A rare blend of brain and heart.

Foremost among them, to me, is a lifelong comrade of mine, to whom has been given the power to write inspired word-picture letters. One of these letters told me of a birding expedition in early May, in North Jersey. I am going to quote part of it. It will appeal to those of you who care not only for birds but for vivid description. Here it is:

"We left home at four in the morning and drove to Troy Meadows, a paradise for ornithologists. There is a broadwalk that goes across the whole marsh, a distance of five miles. We walked to the end and back, and had the most marvelous luck: a view of a least bittern, short-billed marsh wrens and gallinules, all new to me.

"When we started out a fog hung heavy over the marshes. The rising sun would show for a moment, ghostlike, a flat little silver disk, and then be veiled again by the swirl of mists. Out of the blank wall of whiteness all around us came the strange calls of myriads of marsh birds:—

"The whine and the weird diminuendo laugh of the sora,—the heavy unbirdlike grunting of the Virginia rail,—the impersonal metallic tic-tic-tic coming up to us like an uncanny telegraph message from the grebe among the grasses,—the long plaintive cry of some migrating seabird high overhead and flying swiftly,— a confusion of unknown calls punctuated rhythmically by the hollow 'pump' of the bittern.

"When the mists melted and the early morning sun flashed out, the swamp showed in livid green stretches on every side, to the soft blue hills. And the voices of the marsh swelled louder and louder.

"Then all at once the forest birds were awake, too. The air was full of the chorus of thrushes, the high whistle of the cardinals, and the blended warblings of orioles and indigo buntings and rose-breasted gros-beaks. Through it broke the sudden sharp alarm call of a pheasant far off in the woods and the whirring beat of his wings as he rocketed.

"At our feet tiny marsh wrens sang their ecstatic bubbling little song as they clung like animated puff-balls to the tops of the slenderest reeds. Above our heads migrating hawks soared. There were huge herons, too, that seemed to have flown from a Japanese screen. They trailed their flight in long lines, blue gray against the pale green of the swamp."

Does that show technical bird lore or not? It does. Yet it breathes a love of nature and a heart capable of understanding it. Yes, there are ornithologists who see birds as something far more than specimens. This friend of mine proves it. In her name I apologize to the categorists.

And so back to Sunnybank and to our own happy ignorance.

Of all our uncountable (and unclassifiable) winged Sunnybank friends, I like best the catbird. He alone improvises. Most of the others sing the same set of notes over and over, in saccharine repetition. The catbird is not content with that. He makes up his songs as he goes along.

And wonderful songs they are; not reiterations of three or four set tones, but a whole new composition, continuing sometimes for minutes with scarce a duplication throughout. He is not merely a singer. He is a composer. And, like other composers, he is not above stealing what he wants from the songs of less inspired singers. For instance:

There is an oak branch a few yards from our veranda breakfast table. On that branch, morning after morning, a few years ago, a catbird would alight as soon as we sat down to our meal. Never a minute earlier, never a minute later. We could not doubt he had waited for his human audience to arrive before beginning to sing.

He was practicing the four-note call of the oriole.

Slowly and with worried care he would work at it. Sometimes he would get a wrong tone. Then he would stop and go over the whole thing again; keeping it up until he had mastered the song with amazing precision.

With shut eyes, one would have thought an oriole was singing there. Indeed, four different times, during those late May mornings, orioles flew up from the orchard or from the woods or the lawn in response to the call; only to be greeted by the sneeringly triumphant and long-drawn-out catcall of their mimic.

Next he tried to master the song sparrow's trill. That was a failure; and he realized it was. The trill was too much for him. After a day or two he gave up in disgust.

My neighbor, Ernest Gould, told me of seeing a blacksnake running across his lawn, close chased by a thrush whose nest the snake had tried to raid. The next morning, Sunday, as I sat on the Sunnybank veranda, I saw a huge blacksnake wriggle across an oval strip of Sunnybank's lawn which seventy years ago had been used for croquet and which used to be the pride of my father's heart.

Alongside and above and around the snake flapped a furiously irate catbird. The bird was a pal of mine. He and his mate had a nest in a lilac clump, near the house. I had taken much interest in their domestic life and in their three babies. Evidently the blacksnake had been after those babies; and had been driven away by their sire.

Across the smooth-shaven croquet ground they made their way; the two foes. Once and again the snake would try to coil, to strike at his gray-clad pursuer. But always the catbird got out of reach of the blow; and ever he flashed back to the assault, driving the marauder before him.

They crossed the croquet ground and the encircling bit of driveway, and started down the slope of the main lawn which leads to the lake. And now I saw what the blacksnake was seeking to do.

He was making for the long grass of the orchard. There, shielded from direct attack, he could coil at will; and his bird adversary would be fearfully handicapped by the impeding grass stems. The tables would be turned; and the overbold catbird might readily fall prey to his antagonist.

It was time for me to take a hand in the game. As a rule, garter snakes and blacksnakes are not molested at Sunnybank. They do far more good than harm. But now my little gray friend was in danger; and there must be an exception to my rule. I went into action.

I ran after the duelists. I caught up with them just as the snake reached the shelter of the long grass. He turned on his enemy, while the latter was rather badly tangled in the grass meshes. So I ended the battle, by putting my heel on the snake's head.

Then I started back for the veranda. But I did not go alone. Running, hopping, fluttering, the catbird kept close beside me; so close, indeed, that I had to sidestep lest the edges of my hiking boots should bruise him.

I sat down again, on the porch, picking up my Sunday papers. The catbird perched himself on the toe

of the boot which had slain his persecutor. There he
poured forth the sweetest, if the most ridiculous
triumph song imaginable. There could be no shadow of
doubt it was a chant of victory. Almost I could translate
its drift into words. Somewhat along this line:

"I—the all-conquering Catbird—I have slain the
Monster! I drove him from my nest which he invaded!
I pecked him and I battered him with my mighty
pinions as he fled in terror! At the last, I crushed the
very life out of him! (Oh, yes, I admit this large and
slow-moving Human did just a little—a *very* little—to
help me—along toward the end of the struggle; and I
am ready to give him what scant credit is due him.
But the real hero of the fight is my magnificent self!)
All glory be to ME!"

For perhaps ten minutes the vainglorious creature sat
there on my boot-toe or hopped around me, singing at
the top of his lungs his pæan of self-praise. Then he
flew back to his long-neglected nest; perhaps to repeat
to his mate the whole silly boast.

Five times during the next day or so he came again to
the veranda when I was sitting there; and repeated
what seemed to be snatches of his triumph chant. Once
he brought his mate with him. Both perched within a
yard of me, while he sang.

Next to the catbird, I like the song sparrow; the bird
that sends out his spring promise from God on the
rawest and soggiest March day. His a veritable song of
hope.

And, all summer long, he sings it as blithely and

sweetly in the midst of a cloudburst as on a blue-and-gold morning. I am glad he and his clan have chosen me as their friend; and that they come many times a day to the veranda for food.

He—or his mate—has courage, too. One morning, last June, a deluge of rain whipped the porch vines, driven by one of the sudden gales which are part of our North Jersey lake country summer. A song sparrow had built her nest at one side of the veranda. As I was picking up the porch cushions, to toss them out of the path of the rain, I passed several times within a few inches of her nest.

She had flattened herself above her eggs; her wings spread wide, in a effort to shield them from the chill and wet of the storm. Though my hand and arm all but brushed against her and her nest every time I went past her, she did not flinch, nor fly away.

She was looking up at me in an agony of supplication, when at last I chanced to notice her; as if begging me not to destroy her eggs or harm her nest.

I moved far away. The rest of the wet cushions could keep on getting soaked. I was not going to make that piteously huddled bird struggle between terror and mother-care, by continuing to go back and forth, so close to her imperiled eggs.

The wrens are our most self-important guests. Copying, with a dry and wholly non-musical tone, the song sparrow's chants, they have a strut and swagger that are worthier of an Irish terrier or of a giant bird of prey than of such obscure mites. They are without fear. And their home life is a scandal.

In the spring I tack up small boxes or hang small bird houses for them. Usually, by the time I have finished the job and before I can move away, there is a pair of wrens darting forward to take possession. Almost at once they begin the task of weaving their ugly twig-nest.

That is where the domestic squabbles set in. The female will fly away on some errand of her own; leaving the male to find and arrange the twigs. When he has wrought long and wearisomely at it, she comes loafing back. Into the hole of the box or nest she darts. Thence, instantly, comes the sound of strife. She never likes the way her mate has done his work.

Twig after twig she flings out, while he shrieks helpless protests. Then she puts such twigs as are left in such array as she thinks wise; and flies off again, leaving him to continue his dreary labor of collecting another batch of material. This is repeated sometimes for days before she is content with the furnishing of her home; and is ready to settle down in it.

The robin seems to me as much overadvertised in verse and in story as is the horse. Always there are at least two or three robins' nests somewhere in the angles of our veranda. I watch each nest's building, from the moment the female begins to rub her chest along its site to smooth the surface, until it is finished.

Then, after the tiresome incubation, begins the all-day-and-every-day hustle for food for the upturned V-shaped bills of the babies. I don't see how the parent birds keep alive during these feeding weeks. They have not a minute's rest in their work of foraging for their never-satisfied nestlings.

But, if a red squirrel comes along to rifle the nest— or if a young bird falls to the ground—do the parents defend or rescue their offspring? Almost never, in my somewhat long observation years.

Instead, they set up a screaming and a panic-fluttering that lasts for hours. And throughout all the mad hustle and din I have never yet seen one of them do a single practical thing for the imperiled babies. Their song, too, seems to me egregiously overrated; as does the blackbird's. Perhaps I am wrong.

By the way, Will Irwin tells me the American robin is not a robin at all, but some variety of thrush. Irwin says that when the first settlers came here and saw the strange bird, they mistook it for an English robin, by reason of its reddish breast; and that the misused name has stuck.

Once in a blue moon a dog will travel several hundred miles back to his own home. When he does, it is news. And "The Cat Came Back" is a classic. But these are kindergarten feats, alongside the homing flights made by millions of birds every year. The bird flights are miracles. Yet who takes account of them?

A robin will set forth from South Carolina some moonlit night in late March. Straight north he flies, stopping only briefly for food and for rest. Guided by

God-knows-what, he steers a bee-line course which ends when he alights on a corner of the Sunnybank veranda—the same corner wherein he built his nest last year.

Again and again I recognize, by some queer defect or by a smear of atypical color, a bird that has summered for several successive years at Sunnybank. I see him hovering around the same tree or shrub where he nested in earlier summers. From somewhere between Florida and Virginia he has winged from his winter quarters, perhaps a thousand miles, to his summer home.

How did he do it? What incredible twist of brain shaped his course over the chartless airways? To me, it is nature's supreme mystery. And it happens so often that almost nobody thinks about it or stops to figure out a possible clue.

Sometimes, of course, on his night flying he is confused by a glare of light and dashes himself to death against a window pane or a lighthouse along the way. Sometimes, during his short rests, he falls prey to the pot-hunter. But, bar accident, his flight is true and he reaches his goal none the worse for it.

There are other things about our Sunnybank birds that puzzle me. Last year we had almost no orioles in our orchard trees. I did not see three orioles here, though I saw plenty of them within two miles of us.

This season our grounds are full of them; as during all summers except last. Why did they walk out on us last year and why are they all here again now?

For several years we had dozens of big red-headed woodpeckers living in our tree hollows. For the last season or so there has been but a single family of them. Perhaps by next year they will be all over The Place again.

Up to the past twenty years catbirds were rather few, at Sunnybank, except among the waterside willows. Since then they are here in ever-swelling numbers. For which I am more than grateful.

In my boyhood quail were almost as thick-settled here as robins. They used to wander fearlessly all over the lawns and close up to the house. I have heard only one quail on our land during the past thirty years. I wish they would come back.

During the winter, much food is put out every day for our birds. Especially when the snow lies deep. At such times patches of ground are shoveled clean and the provender is put there. This has led to something else I can't understand:

There will not be a bird in sight when the seeds and crumbs and suet are strewn in the bare spots. Yet within three minutes a bevy of them will have arrived—from where?—for the feast. How did they know?

I will take a handful of grain and pour it on the veranda floor, at the opposite side of the house from where the birds are feeding. Almost immediately I will see some of those same birds—not newcomers but the same feasters—crowding around the grain on the porch. How do they know it is there? They cannot see it. The wind is in the wrong direction, so they cannot smell it. But they find it at once. How?

On my hikes I have seen flocks of blackbirds feeding in buckwheat stubble, with a sentinel bird perched on a tree. As I drew closer the sentinel's head would go up and his black throat would swell in a warning call that sent his comrades up into the air in a whirring cloud.

Twice, by a simple feat of stalking, I have been able to creep up on the sentinel bird, so that I was only a few yards from him when he discovered me. As usual his head went up and his throat swelled in that warning call. Close as I was to him, I could not hear a sound. Yet birds feeding in hollows, two hundred feet away, heard it and flew for safety. These birds had been out of sight of the sentry and they must have reacted only to the sound of his call.

I had heard nothing. Thus I know blackbirds have in their voices notes which are so high or so low as to be inaudible to humans, though easily heard and understood by one another. High or low notes and a correspondingly geared sense of hearing, of which we know nothing.

I did not invent the theory or the experiment I have described. I read of the test, many years ago, in something written by Ambrose Bierce. Then I tried it out at Sunnybank. And I found it true.

Bierce went a step further by hinting that if certain bird-and-animal sounds are beyond the range of the human ear, so there may be creatures whose coloring renders them invisible to mankind, though seen by bird and beast. He made this fantastic notion account for a cat's arching its back and spitting at something its master cannot see; for a dog growling or cringing at an unseen something; for a flock of chickens squawking and scattering when no hawk is in the sky above them.

I have seen often these phenomena of the cat and the dog and the chickens. So have you. But I don't think there is any use in diving into the occult to explain them. However, I have proved Bierce's claim that some birds have notes too high or too low to register in the human ear. Which is just one more of the countless bird mysteries I cannot hope to fathom.

They are as methodical as an elderly bookkeeper, these Sunnybank birds. We can tell to within a space of three days at most when the vanguard of each separate species will arrive on its northerly flight. To within a day or so when the nesting will begin and when the second brood will be started. Then, to within almost the same space of time, when the birds will vanish in a body.

I don't mean when they flock and make ready to fly south. That does not come until long after the "vanishing" and there is nothing secretive about their preparations for the October trip. But, in late summer one realizes that the hundreds of song-birds are not only silent but are gone.

They have slipped into the deepest woods, far from the haunts of man, for the solemn rite of moulting and of starting the pinfeathers for their next plumage.

Whether from shame or from feeling ill or from what-soever unexplained cause, they want to get out of the way, out of sight. A few hang on, but most of them are in the forest thickets; mute, miserable, incurably shy.

At Pompton, more than a half century ago—long before the once-slumberous old village was renamed Pompton Lakes—a teacher came to the district school, some two miles from Sunnybank; a teacher who was a forerunner of the whole modern race of Linnæans and of other Audubon devotees. She craved to awaken in her little pupils a love for birds and a better compre-hension of them.

With this in view, she inaugurated a system of prizes to be awarded to children who should see and classify aright the largest number of local birds on their way to school on spring mornings. With zeal the youngsters threw themselves into the competition.

One of them, I remember, sought to enlarge his day's meager list by incorporating into it a cassowary and two ostriches and a great auk and six flamingoes. Loud were his laments and his charges of favoritism when that morning's prize went to a tow-headed brat whose score was only three robins and a house wren and a song sparrow and a crow.

I remember dear teacher used to give sugary talks about the birds, just before recess—talks fringed with saccharine questions to one pupil after another. The only one of her ornithology queries I recall today stuck in my youthful memory because of the reply it brought forth.

Teacher cooed to Manny Tod—who roused our envy later by a deserved promotion to the reform school at Trenton—this sweet appeal:

"Now, Manny, don't you just love the pretty robins hopping all over the grass out there?"

"Yes'm," dubiously answered Manny Tod. "Only *I* can't never seem to hit the damn things!"

Not very interesting, was it, this digression about dear teacher's futile bird propaganda? I brought it in only to let Linnæans know how valiantly and how vainly their forerunners wrought to spread the bird gospel among the rustics.

By prosy degrees, back again to the birds of Sunnybank; at least to the last bird I shall bother you with. He is worth a word or two, I think. For he was such a pest that I was sore tempted to break my rule against the firing of a gun on The Place.

Above the biggest puppy-yard juts an oak limb. Some years ago, and in the very middle of a bright day, a fist-sized screech owl appeared from nowhere in particular and perched on that branch. Blinking down at the eight half-grown collie pups that lived in the yard, the little owl began to hoot.

The puppies gathered in a hushed semicircle, just beneath him; sitting on their haunches and with their muzzles pointing upward. They listened with awed reverence to his quavering song.

As soon as the owl paused for breath, all eight young collies broke into a wild uproar of barking. Then, of a sudden, they fell silent; and the owl would continue his long-drawn hoots. Again he would pause for breath; and again the wild chorus of barks answered him.

This went on, back and forth, for perhaps half an hour. There was something eerie about the whole thing; a ghastly likeness to the responsive readings in church.

The owl flew away, at last; only to come back again the next noon, and on every midday for an entire fortnight. Daily, the plangently nerve-teasing "responsive readings" went on for half an hour or so.

Then the horrible bird came back no more. I like to hope someone shot him. He and his eight collie acolytes had interfered hideously with my work.

CHAPTER SEVEN

Sunnybank's "Little People"

WHEN my daughter was a child, she spoke of Sunnybank's birds and non-canine animals as "the Little People." The name stuck.

One of these Little People was not little at all, but more than sixteen hands high. And he lived to be thirty-six years old. He was our chestnut gelding, Fritz. His dam was my father's old saddle mare, Belle, bought when I was ten.

From the time Fritz was a wabbly-legged colt, he was given the run of the grounds here. This, until he was saddle-and-harness broke at the age of four.

On the same principle that a housedog is humanized fiftyfold more than is a kennel-pent pup, Fritz's daily association with us gave him a queer wisdom and a whimsical sense of fun.

He would come at my whistle, as readily as would any collie. But seldom did he wait for that whistle.

I had taught him to eat lumps of sugar. He knew I was likely to have sugar in my pockets. So at sight or scent or sound of my presence, whenever I came outdoors, he would gallop up to me, nosing for the treat he loved.

Often he would be grazing at the top of the hill near the road—then a shaded country lane—and he would come tearing down the steepest part of the slope at breakneck speed.

Avoiding the countless big trees in his path and hurling the boulders, he would keep that whirlwind pace until his nose was perhaps eighteen inches from my chest. Then he would halt with incredible suddenness and begin to nuzzle for sugar or for pipe tobacco.

How he could stop so instantly and without sliding, I don't know. It was a trick all his own. The thunderous downhill rush used to terrify guests who happened to be with me. But never once did the colt overstep his halting place by so much as an inch.

Having munched the sugar lump or the palmful of tobacco, he did not go his way. Graft was only a part of his reason for seeking me out in that tumultuous fashion. He loved me.

As long as I might wander about The Place, he kept at my side; once in a while lashing out playfully at me with unshod hoofs that never reached their mark; or seizing my shoulder or elbow between jaws which could have crushed my bones and which did not exert pressure of half a pound.

He and I enjoyed those rambles, mightily. The one drawback was that he followed me up on the veranda when I went into the house and he tried to squeeze in at the door. That would call for a rebuke which he took with hypocritical meekness—repeating the same stunt at the end of our next walk.

I had a roan saddle horse, The Don, during Fritz's colthood. The Don was as large for a horse as I was for a man. He was a ganglion of crazily high-strung nerves. He took a lot of watchful riding, because of this acute nervousness. I never could be off-guard while I was on his back.

But the worst times I had with The Don were when Fritz chanced to be at large as we came in at the gateway on our return home. Always when I was going for a ride, I shut Fritz into an enclosed shed which was his sleeping place. But more than once he pushed the door down or joggled open its fastening.

Freed, he would gallop up the driveway to meet The Don and myself. He would frisk madly around us, nipping my horse's hips, yanking at his tail or tempting him right successfully to start on a mad race through the thickest of the trees.

This kind of thing drove The Don wild. It was all I could do to keep him from bolting. He and I would have one continuous battle for mastery all the way down to the stables, Fritz capering gleefully about us and adding his humble share to the fun. With a holy joy, at such times, I could have shot him.

Once, when I was starting for a ride, I told the coachman to see that Fritz did not get out of his shed while I was gone and, if he should work himself free, to shut him up in one of the stable's stalls.

On my way homeward I ran into such a rain-driving

tornado as scourges our North Jersey lake country at times in June. I had all I could do to prevent The Don from running amuck through blind terror and to keep him in the road.

As we turned in at the gates, Fritz came pattering up ecstatically for a glad romp with us. He had worked his way out of the shed. The men had not chanced to see him.

By this time the cloudburst and the gale had died as suddenly as they had begun. The air was crystal clear and it was golden with late afternoon sunlight.

I was drenched to the skin. My arms ached from my long tussle with The Don. I was not minded to have an encore performance of the snorting horse's road antics.

So I dismounted. Leading The Don by the rein and Fritz by the forelock, I started to walk down to the house, amid a strew of storm-torn branches and leaves and twigs.

Halfway down the slope I chanced to look toward the stables and to Fritz's shed just behind them. A giant basswood tree had been uprooted by the tornado. It had crashed down upon the shed, flattening it as thoroughly as a ton weight would flatten a cardboard box.

If Fritz had not got out when he did he would have been crushed to death.

When his course of breaking was ended, he developed into an ideal saddle-and-driving horse. But never, when he was loose, did he give up the habit of following me everywhere. Also, he carried his queer sense of fun into his work.

He would change from a jog-trot to a runaway gallop when one least expected it. Before the driver or rider could brace himself to fight against the runaway's bolt, Fritz had calmed down again to sedateness. This of his own accord. The gallop never continued for more than about fifteen yards at most.

Many times he would dart sideways as some woman or man plodded past us on the road. With a deft twist he would jerk the pedestrian's hat off, toss it to the farther side of the highway and then continue his demure progress.

It was not easy to be on guard against this idiotic prank of his. For sometimes he would go for months without playing it. I had to pay two women for ruined hats and to endure horrible objurgations from practically all the headgear-denuded victims.

To the Mistress alone Fritz was wholly prankless and docile. From the day I lifted her from the porch and carried her across the threshold and in through the front doorway of Sunnybank House (another old North Jersey custom, now forgotten) when we came back from our wedding trip Fritz adored her. Never would he bolt while she was driving him. Nor would he disgrace her by snatching off the hats of passers-by.

But he imposed on her, most arrantly. He would not stir from the horse block until she had given him his morning lumps of sugar. He didn't balk. He just stood there.

And sometimes on their drives he pretended to be too exhausted to move faster than a crawling walk. Well he knew she would not lash him out of his slowness. Presently, when he had played the silly game long enough to suit him, he would set out again at a brisk trot.

Only once did the Mistress bring down the whip on Fritz's back with any vehemence. She was driving him over to the station one moonlight night—long before we bought our first car—to bring me home. She was driving a Concord buggy, a roomy vehicle with a sort of platform at the back for carrying a trunk.

Fritz chose that time to slow down to a pseudo-weary walk. A man was shuffling along at the road-side. The moon cast his shadow on the ground as the Mistress happened to glance sidewise. She saw from the shadow that he had broken into a run.

Then there was a jarring of the buggy and the shadow showed he had swung himself up on the platform and was rising to his feet, tugging at the leather tags which fastened the rear curtain.

The Mistress smote Fritz a swashing blow across the loins with the whip, just as the man was trying to get his balance. The horse gave a mighty bound forward, well-nigh snapping the traces. There was a howl from the man, followed instantly by a loud thud as his head hit the road.

When we came past the same place on the way home, I got out and hunted the wayside grass for sign of him. But he had been able to get away.

After that, I insisted the Mistress carry a pistol when she drove over to the station for me. She was a splendid shot, with both rifle and revolver. Yet she would not promise to tote the pistol along until I showed her it was loaded only with blank cartridges.

I bade her fire low, for the abdomen, if ever she had to shoot; and I explained to her that the harmless report of the blank cartridge would scare away anyone who might try to molest her.

Then, secretly, I dumped out the blanks and re-loaded the heavy caliber pistol with ball cartridges. Luckily, she never had need of it.

When Fritz was twenty-five years old, we had his shoes taken off—for a long time he had been doing only the very lightest of work—and I promised him he need never again feel the touch of bit or of shoe.

Henceforth he was Sunnybank's honored pensioner. In summer he dwelt in a big paddock. In winter he had a roomy boxstall from whose window he was eternally looking forth in all directions with keen interest.

Every day he had a handful of sugar. Every day we came down to paddock or stall to see him. He had a wonderful old age. Little by little, as the years went on, his once-level backbone began to sag. There were gray hairs above his eyes. But his head was as classically beautiful as always it had been.

Then one morning when he was thirty-six years old, we found him dead in his stall.

He was the last of the Sunnybank horses. Why should we batter a horse's feet and spring his knees and risk collision with a fool-driven motor car, by taking him out on the the concrete highway? The horse has no place, except as a draft animal, in these speed-mad days.

When we want haying done, we hire a team by the day. When we want to drive comfortably behind a horse or to ride horseback, we go to almost motorless Bermuda.

As Fritz was the largest of Sunnybank's long-lived Little People, so Jack was the smallest. Though, for his kind, Jack waxed somewhat enormous during his twenty years with us.

In 1912 we built—or dug—a lily-and-goldfish pool in the woods; a pool that always has been the joy of the Mistress's heart. She has spent years in beautifying it and its surroundings.

As soon as the pool was filled with water we stocked it with goldfish and tadpoles and miniature turtles, and planted varicolored waterlilies in it.

One of that first year's crop of tadpoles met with disaster almost as soon as his tail changed to a pair of green legs. I don't know what happened to him. Whatever it was it left him with one eye clouded over with white film and with a triangular white scar on the top of his head.

I speak of his disfigurement, that you may see we could not possibly mistake him for any other frog.

The Mistress named him "Jack." She made rather a pet of him, feeding flies to him and scratching his back. He was as tame as any of the dogs.

By the time he was two or three years old, he used to

climb up into the pool's waste pipe and sit there croaking. It sounded as though he were croaking through a megaphone. A most creditably reverberant croak. He seemed proud of it.

Every October he would burrow deep into the mud at the bottom of the pool. Every spring, on the first warm day, he would come back to the surface.

By and by he grew too big for the waste pipe. So he had to do his croaking in the open. It must have humiliated him to find he could croak no louder than any of his poolmates, now that he had no megaphonic help.

He lived on, always recognizable by his perfect tameness as well as by the three-cornered white scar and the white-filmed right eye. Slowly but steadily he kept on growing. He waxed huge.

But never did he become half so large as one or two of the bullfrogs I have seen in the lake's weeds. A few of those wild bullfrogs must have been fully half a century old. I judge this by their size in comparison with Jack's.

He came out of his hibernation as usual in April of 1932. That spring he was a full twenty years old, to our knowledge. We hailed his return from the mud as that of an old friend.

In mid-May we went on our annual spring pilgrimage to the Berkshires. When we came home Jack had vanished.

Next day I found his car-flattened body just outside the Sunnybank gates, on the highroad; more than a furlong from the pool.

The whitened eye and the triangular head scar identified the smashed corpse beyond all doubt. But how in the name of all that is impossible did he get to the road?

Never before, to the best of my belief, had he strayed six feet from the home pool. Why should he have hopped uphill a furlong and in the opposite direction from the lake or any other body of water?

The answer is: He didn't. At least I am wholly certain he didn't. I think I know the solution to the puzzle:

When we are here, the Sunnybank gates are shut and the "No Admittance Today" sign is fastened to them, at ten o'clock in the morning. This, so that we can get a modicum of uninterrupted work done and so that we may not be overrun all day by motor tourists. But when we are away from home the gates are allowed to stand open much of the time.

If motorists really must trespass, let it be in our absence. And they do. They come here in swarms to look over the non-spectacular Place and to see the dogs. One of our men goes around with them—almost never getting a tip for his trouble—to keep them from doing any damage.

My theory is that one of a sightseeing batch of motorists passed by the pool on the way from the kennels and saw old Jack squatting on the brink, sunning himself; that he scooped up the tame frog and carried it to the car with him. Perhaps as a Sunnybank souvenir, perhaps in quest of frog legs.

Then when he got to the main road he decided the

prize was not worth his lugging it around all day in his pockets; and he pitched it out on the ground as so many tons of motorist-stolen spring flowers and shrubs are pitched out of cars every day. Either the fall killed Jack or else the next car's wheel squashed over him.

We miss our queer green friend. He is oddly missable after those twenty years of acquaintanceship.

I don't count the pool's goldfish among our Little People. To me they are as uninteresting as they are ornamental. Yet they puzzle me.

One November I take half of them into the house and put them into the aquarium. The other half I leave to winter at the bottom of the pool. The next spring I find all the aquarium fish have died and all those in the pool are alive.

The next November I do the same thing. The following spring finds all the aquarium fish in fine condition and all the pool's fish dead. It doesn't make sense. But neither do the goggle-eyed fish, themselves.

One year's poolful of goldfish will dart in and out among the Mistress's fingers when she dabbles her hand in the pool. The next year's fish will scurry away in a splashing delirium of terror if one of us comes within a yard of them.

Silly illogical things, at best. But they are rather pretty as they loaf among the colored lily blossoms. So we go on buying a few of them every season, to replace the winter's casualties.

Caruso and Melba rated high among our Little People. So to a lesser degree, did their predecessor, Simon Peter Rhadames. All three were peacocks.

Simon Peter Rhadames passed out of the picture after a single year. He didn't like us and he didn't like Sunnybank. He was a morose fowl. And presently he went the way of all flesh. Personally, I think "he only died to spite us."

His place was taken—and vastly improved on—by gorgeous Caruso and his dove-colored mate, Melba. We had them for years. They were our good friends. They would follow us majestically on our walks through the rose garden and over the lawns. They were tame, too. The Mistress could pat them, at will, and they seemed to enjoy it. She has a mystic "way" with animals and birds, which I lack.

At five o'clock, every afternoon, in those days, tea was served on the veranda. In almost no time Caruso and Melba learned to know the precise hour. Wherever they might be they would come to the foot of the porch steps and stand there in grave expectancy, till bits of cake or of buttered toast were thrown to them.

Now here is an odd thing about that habit of theirs: As soon as we went to New York in late autumn, both peacocks would go up the hill and spend the winter near the gate lodge. Apparently they craved human companionship. My superintendent told me he never saw them wandering around Sunnybank House during our absence.

At that time we spent five months a year at our Riverside Drive flat—our Flat of Winter Exile, as we have named it. On the first day of our return to Sunnybank in early spring, the two peacocks would appear at the foot of the veranda, precisely at five o'clock. There they would stand, as on the year before, waiting for their scraps of cake and toast.

Spring after spring they would do that. They had either grand memories or an acute sense of the smell of tea.

During our Sunnybank sojourn, Melba roosted always in the top of a tall fir tree near the house. Caruso's bedroom was the highest bough of an apple tree in the orchard. On bright moonlit nights he would sound his cracked trumpet call every hour. Always at dawn, he and Melba would squawk a long-range good morning to each other from their respective treetops.

One spring Melba nested in the deep grass under a maple tree in our upper meadow across the highway. In due time she picked her way back down the hill to the house, followed by five partridge-colored baby peafowl. By a minor miracle no car killed them as they crossed the road.

Caruso was effusively glad to see Melba at home again. He had moped in her absence of several weeks. He accepted the five babies as friends and he helped to forage for them. For weeks in the early summer, life was wonderfully pleasant for the peacock family. The chicks grew apace. Soon each of them had a perky little feather topknot. They began to look like peafowl seen through the small end of a field glass.

It was pretty to watch Melba's care of them and her efforts to educate them. The foremost of these educational efforts was to teach them to roost with her at night on the rooftree of the stables. (From earliest babyhood they had roosted on the easily climbed top of the root cellar. Never on the ground.)

To reach the stable-crest there is a simple method. One need only take a short flight to the one-story top of the winter kennels. Thence, one may walk precariously up the steepish roof of the original barn's peaked woodshed. Thence to the stable roof is a flight of some seven feet.

Melba would fly to the kennel roof, chuckling and crooning to urge her children to follow her. One by one, fluttering like quail, they obeyed. It was little trouble to guide them to the top of the higher woodshed. Then the real education began. Melba would fly thence to the peak of the stable roof. There she would lean far over and croon encouragement to the five chicks that stood below and peered miserably and hopelessly up at her.

Not a chick stirred. Melba flew back to her brood. Again she flew to the stable's ridgepole. This time one daring chick followed. She kept flying back and forth, chick after chick timorously following her return ascent.

It was perhaps an hour before she had coaxed the timid last of them to join her on the dizzy summit. She must have been tired, to the very bone. But next night each and every chick joined her unhesitatingly in her flight. They learned quickly and easily, once they had started to learn.

When the babies were about two months old they began to show a greenish sheen around their throats and chests. They were several times larger than when they had been hatched. We had heard that peachicks were hard to raise. Thus far we had had no trouble at all with them.

One day, Caruso was wandering alone near the road almost a quarter-mile from the house. A neighbor's young son had a new target rifle. From the porch the Mistress and I heard the nasty spitting crack of this petty weapon.

A minute later we saw Caruso in all the splendor of his full plumage walking slowly yet majestically down the slope toward us. Straight on he came, swerving for nothing, until he was close to the Mistress.

Then, very quietly, he slumped to the ground below her feet, stone-dead. There was a 22-caliber rifle ball through his column of iridescent throat.

Hesitantly, Melba picked her way forward to where he had tumbled. Long she stood above his still body, bending now and then to touch it with her beak.

Disconsolate, she moved away. Thenceforth she would eat nothing. Within ten days she had pined herself to death through grief for her resplendent dead mate.

One by one the orphaned chicks sickened and died, in spite of all we could do for them. Thus ended our last experiment in peacock raising.

Among the Little People I must include two of our many successive cows.

One of them was a priceless registered Guernsey given us by Colonel Kuser. Peggy was the lovablest and friendliest cow I have known. Like old Fritz, she would come at my call and would follow me everywhere. We had her for three years before she sickened and died. In her stomach was found imbedded a sharp-pointed nail which somehow had got into her feed.

She was beautiful, a grand milker and of tremendous cash value. But none of those elements was responsible for the unhappiness that was ours at her death.

The second and less worth-while cow was Imogene, named for the black heifer in *The Wizard of Oz*.

Up to her fourth year black Imogene was as gentle as a kitten. My wife and daughter used to fasten tricolor ribbons to her horns on Independence Day. Imogene was frankly proud of the decorations. She was that kind of cow.

Then, on May thirtieth, 1914, occurred something which I am going to tell you; although I don't believe a word of it.

I was in New York, at work. Imogene was tethered by a long iron chain in the lush grass of the springtime hillside woods.

Up came a furious little thunderstorm. A crash of thunder and a blinding pink flash of lightning enlivened things, just as my superintendent and one of my men were on their way to lead Imogene to the cow shed.

They found the young cow lying on her side and thrashing wildly about in the undergrowth. Not a hair was left on her tail.

The men declared that the lightning bolt had hit her on the tail, stripping it of hair. That is manifestly absurd. A lightning bolt which smote the cow in the tail would have killed her. Whereas in ten minutes Imogene was as well as ever.

What happened, I think, was that the remnants of a lightning stroke glanced off from whatever tree it may have hit and ran along her steel chain. Imogene may have been lying down at the time and her tail may have been touching the chain. Of course that is only a guess. But it is the only plausible guess I can make.

But this I *do* know: From that day and during the next four years, until we sold her for beef, gentle Imogene had the temper of a sick wildcat. It was not safe for anyone to handle her. And she was threefold more virulent toward women than toward men.

Stranger still, as any farmer will understand, during those four years she continued to give daily quantities of milk—excellent milk as befitted her half-Alderney parentage—and never once did she have a calf. To you who are familiar with dairy matters, that phenomenon will seem far more unusual than the alleged stripping of her tail by lightning.

At last she waxed so increasingly dangerous that I sold her to a butcher. She had long since ceased to qualify as one of our Little People.

Today we have but two cows—all we need. Neither of them rates as one of the Little People. They are Inez and Boadicea, the Ice Cream Cow and the Dog Cow.

Inez is three parts Alderney. Her milk is rich. Her cream is butter-thick. It serves as basis for our ice cream and mousse and for the finer elements of cooking.

Boadicea, the huge hornless black Holstein with map borders on her big sides, gives more and thinner milk than does Inez; milk which suffices for all the uses of our kennels. Hence the designations: Ice Cream Cow and Dog Cow.

Up to a few years ago we averaged some forty-five grown registered collies in our kennels and usually from two to four litters of puppies. We needed all of Boadicea's milk.

But the motor world wore a path to our door in bringing such swarms that we cut down the size of the kennels to a very few dogs, chiefly ragged old pensioners which had given us grand service in their day, and to perhaps a single litter of puppies a year. Soon our kennels may be empty.

Motorists grew to regarding The Place as a blend of zoo and picnic grove, and me as a disgusted freak to be queried and stared at.

One Sunday noon as we drove home from church, the Mistress spoke of the inhospitable look of the closed iron gates and of the "No Admittance Today" sign. She asked me to leave the gates open. I did.

During the next two hours thirty-five cars—I counted them—bumped down the drive. All of them were crammed with strangers who had no claim on us. They cut the turf at the drive's edges. Their children hurled pebbles and sticks at the friendly puppies which trotted hospitably forward to the wire walls of the yards to greet them. Their women ripped up rosebushes by the roots—the flowers are to the Mistress what the dogs are to me—and in less mentionable ways they made themselves pleasingly at home.

They and their men started to build no fewer than three picnic fires against the trunks of our largest and most ancient oaks. Men spat tobacco juice on the concrete floor of the porch. Men and their female mates and their young reached in through open windows and doors and stole seven books from tables and shelves.

At the end of two hours I telephoned to the lodge, ordering the gates shut. It was our last experiment in indiscriminate hospitality.

Which is an intemperate digression. And so back to the Sunnybank Little People:

Our seventy pigeons, all but one, are snow-white. They make a pretty picture, feeding on our green lawns or in spring amid the green hillside's great masses of golden daffodils.

They sleep in cotes on the side of the stable, where they quarrel fiercely and in every way prove the fallacy of a dove's gentleness.

I have read that domestic pigeons never roost on

trees. But at feeding time the oak limbs above our kennel yards are white with the clouds of pigeons waiting impatiently to swoop down and raid the collies' dinner dishes.

I don't suppose the snowy flock has a single redeeming trait, beyond providing us now and then with squabs. But a flight of gleaming white pigeons circling against a blue sky above a blue lake and with living green beyond them is a spectacle worth the theft of a little dog-food.

Besides, there is another element to my keeping them. Three months before my family moved from Springfield, Massachusetts, to Brooklyn, in October of 1884, Ed Smith and I levied a forced loan on the key to the belfry of the First Congregational Church. We crept up there at dead of night and stole great bagfuls of the pigeons which roosted amid the creaky scaffolding.

I chose as my share fourteen of the whitest pigeons and I brought them here to Sunnybank. The freight charge, I remember, was $1.20. They were the ancestors of my great white flock. The Sunnybank doves are as tame as chickens; a fault which leads to the occasional killing of one of them by some dinner-defrauded dog or by cat or rat.

A few red squirrels have merited at least brevet rank among our Little People. There are years when the grounds are overrun by them. Again, for several seasons, we see only one or two. Engaging little pests they are. They do quite as much damage as the rats.

Yet one traps or shoots a rat; and one grins tolerantly at a squirrel. It is all a matter of personality.

As a college lad I used to do vacation studying far down in the woods where I had rigged a hammock. On the way thither I would go through the orchard and pick up apples, to lighten my scholastic chores. Almost at once three red squirrels discovered me. They would climb out on branches over my head and chatter defiance. Or they would creep cautiously down the tree trunk until they were close to me; then rush back again in noisy nerve-rack.

I used to toss bits of apple to them. At first with exaggerated caution, then in no fear at all, they would snatch up the gifts. Usually they carried the apple slices to the branch just above me and dropped the chewed fragments of skin on my head.

As the season wore on, my three red playmates lost all fear of me—they had had no shred of respect for me from the outset—and they would climb or drop into the hammock and eat slices of apple out of my hand. Always they ran forward to meet me as I came to the edge of the woods, and escorted me to my seat.

Then I went to town. When I came back for a week-end my trio of rufous chums were gone.

Cecil deMille lived about half a mile away. He was a schoolboy in those days. He told me gleefully that he had gone hunting in the Sunnybank woods and that three red squirrels came scampering toward him unafraid. He got all three with one shot.

Fritz Van de Water is surpassingly wise, besides being supreme good company. Never did he say a wiser thing than: *"When you tame a wild creature you sign its death warrant."*

Last summer two red squirrels were orphaned or else abandoned at an age when they still should have been in their nest. They set forth on their own. They were mostly head and tail, with bodies barely two inches long. They chose the lawn, close to the house, as their hunting ground.

The Mistress and I were at breakfast on the veranda when the three dogs—Sandy and Chips and Beth—that lay beside the table, jumped to their feet and charged merrily at something on the lawn. It was one of the impossibly tiny squirrels. I yelled to them to come back. With much reluctance they obeyed. So—with no reluctance at all—did the squirrel.

At sound of my shout, the squirrel started toward me at a shambling gallop. By the time I had ordered the dogs indoors, he had reached the foot of the veranda. Up a vine he swarmed awkwardly and thence to a post. This brought him within six inches of my hand. He seemed overjoyed to have found such nice friends.

I had difficulty to keep him from hopping onto the table and into my plate. With greedy zest he nibbled at the bit of cantaloupe I offered him, and then at a red raspberry. He accepted a piece of toast less eagerly, but with relish. That was the beginning.

Day after day he and his brother—or she and her

sister, whichever it was—came scuttling across the lawn to us as soon as we sat down to breakfast or to lunch on the veranda. Up the vines they clambered and sought to eat from our plates.

Their parents had left them too early to implant in the youngsters the normal fear of man. They were not afraid of anything at all. They followed the laundress about the drying ground on wash days, getting under her feet, trying to climb her skirt. This, I suppose, because the maids as well as ourselves had taken to feeding the two orphans.

Then, one morning, they were gone. Perhaps they had decided to become self-supporting and to live henceforth in the woods. I want to think so.

Far likelier they had been killed by dog or cat or rat or hawk or crow; another pathetic example of Van de Water's maxim on the cruelty of taming the Wild.

I shall do no more than touch the high spots of the generations of cats and of kittens which have held merited rank among our Little People:

Eyolf, the stable cat which used to insist on going with me on three-mile hikes through snow and rain and two-inch slush at dead of winter, refusing to be left behind—Juliet which brought me daily every variety of food from gory rats to chipmunks, laying them at my feet and crooning motherwise an urgent invitation for me to devour them; Juliet which actually swam out ten yards or more into the lake after my boat, several mornings in succession—Peter Grimm that slept at the foot of my bed for five years and at last met death under a motor car's tires as he was following me across the highroad toward one of our woodland rambles—Tippy, born April 6, 1915, just two years before the day Uncle Sam celebrated her anniversary by declaring war on Germany; and died October 30, 1930, the temperamental gray Persian cat which belonged to the Mistress and for more than fifteen years was a fluffily unsparable part of our home life; a furry little comrade still keenly missed—these and a score of others.

(A goodly number of newspapers, last year, denounced me as a cat-hater, hinting I had not the heart nor the intelligence or breadth to appreciate any creature but a dog. A horde of wistful little furry ghosts could have given them the lie.)

I have but scratched the surface of our Sunnybank Little People's endless roster. Perhaps I have written uninterestingly of them—at any rate I have not so much as mentioned our long line of glorious dogs—but no book dealing with Sunnybank would be half-way complete without a few pages devoted to them.

Some of the Little People did not mean much to the Mistress nor to me. Others were absurdly dear to us and are hard to forget.

So many of us humans live too long. But all animals die too soon.

CHAPTER EIGHT

Sunnybank's Canine Ghost

THIS story is to be believed by you or not, as you may prefer. If you'll read it, you will note that I don't go on record as to my own belief or non-belief. In the hard-to-credit parts of it I cite the testimony of other people; including that of a minister of the gospel and of a shrewd business man.

These two men did not know each other; never had heard of each other. Both of them were my friends, men whose truthfulness I would gamble on. I had known them well for more than twenty years.

Nor would it have been at all possible for them to get together to plan a stupid hoax. For, as I have just told you, neither of them had heard of the other.

Also, if you ask me if I believe in ghosts, my only honest answer must be:

"I don't know anything about the subject. I have lived too long and seen too much, to laugh as heartily as once I could at any strange thing I can't explain. I have not made a study of psychology nor of psychical phenomena. I am not greatly interested in such themes."

I have listened to numberless ghost stories, some of them told with an aggressive defiance little short of ferocity—a fierce challenge to the listener to dare deny or deride—others recounted in evident fear of being laughed at or of being set down as a liar or loose-geared mentally. The topic seems to admit of no compromise, no middle ground of agreement.

In England I saw a dreary farce-comedy with one redeeming flash of dialogue. The play was called *Thark*. An elderly bore is trying to convince his nephew that there are no such things as ghosts. He demands:

"Did you ever see a ghost?"

"Not yet," is the reluctant answer.

"Ever know anyone who had seen a ghost?"

"No. But everyone, whom I know, has known someone who's seen a ghost."

And so to our story:

I have told this tale to three or four people. One of them nodded approval and said:

"With a snappy climax it might work up into a good yarn. But your imagination seems to have slumped, halfway through it."

Of the others, one looked polite; a second said something vague about "fish stories."

So I have scant encouragement to tell it again. However, I am going to take a chance. As I said, I don't ask you to believe it and I am not on record as saying whether or not *I* believe it. I am merely going to tell it to you in the form of a group of disconnected facts and let you draw your own conclusions from them.

I am not going to link up those facts into anything or air any theories. I have no theories on them. I cite nothing *I* may or may not have thought I experienced. But I affirm the truth of the set of statements I am going to make.

Fact Number One—We had a giant crossbreed dog, here at Sunnybank. His name was Rex.

He was larger than a collie; and he had short, fawn-colored hair. He was the only short-haired dog at Sunnybank after the death of my daughter's bull-terrier, Paddy. Perhaps you read about Rex in the final story of my book, *Lad: A Dog*. In that I told of his death-battle with old Laddie in the snowchoked forests behind Sunnybank.

Rex, from earliest puppyhood, was my slavishly devoted worshiper. Everywhere I went, he followed. If I changed from one chair to another, Rex would get up, quietly, and move over to where I sat; curling up on the floor close beside my chair and looking at me.

Almost never, when I was in sight, did he take his eyes from my face.

He was not allowed in the dining room. So, at meal times, he took up his stand always just outside the long French window behind my chair and peered in at me.

Bear those petty things in mind, won't you?—his habit of curling up at my feet, with his eyes fixed on me, and of standing outside the long window of the dining room, looking steadfastly in at me. They come strongly into the story again, both of them.

Also, when I was not around, his favorite drowsing place was a patch of floor to the left of the door of my study. For years, he used to lie there. Remember that, too, please.

Rex was killed.

That was in March of 1916.

Fact Number Two—In the autumn of 1917, Henry A. Healy, a high official of the so-called Leather Trust, spent the evening with us. We sat in front of the big fireplace in the living room, warming ourselves at the blaze.

This guest, by the way, was a level-headed man, not given to queer fancies or to hallucinations. He had been mildly amused, in other years, at Rex's devotion to me, and by the big crossbreed's freak ancestry (collie and bull-terrier) and by his odd physique. He had seen Rex again and again.

As Healy and I were standing in the hallway while he put on his ulster, late in the evening, he said:

"I wish some animal cared as much for me as Rex cares for you. I was watching him, for half an hour tonight, curled close beside your chair in front of the hearth, and staring so adoringly up into your face. He——"

"Good Lord man!" I sputtered. "Rex has been dead for more than a year. You know that."

He looked blankly at me, for a moment. Then, as if in a daze, he mumbled:

"Why—why, so he has! I had clean forgotten!

Just the same," he added, the blank look on his face deepening, "*I saw him lying on the floor beside you, all this evening!*"

Fact Number Three—In the summer of 1918, the Reverend Appleton Grannis, who had been in college with me, came to spend a week at Sunnybank. He had been away from this part of the country for a long time. It was his first visit to Sunnybank in several years.

He had never seen Rex. He had never heard of Rex. He did not know Healy. Indeed, to the best of my belief, he knew none of the guests who had been at Sunnybank in recent years.

He and I were sitting together in the dining room one hot afternoon trying to counteract the outer heat by copious internal applications of ice-cold beer.

I sat as usual with my back to the long window. Grannis was facing me.

As we got up to leave the room, he asked me:

"What is the name of the dog that has been standing out there on the veranda looking in at you through the window?"

"Was it Lad?" I hazarded. "It may have been Bruce or Wolf or——"

"No," he corrected me, impatiently. "It wasn't any of those. It was a dog I haven't seen here before. A great big short-haired dog—not long-coated like the rest of yours. He wasn't a collie. He had a fawn-colored coat; a coat as short as a bull-terrier's. And a crooked scar across his nose. He spent the best part of an hour just standing there and watching you. He's gone now. Which dog is he?"

"I—don't know," I answered with entire truthfulness.

Fact Number Four—I have told you that Rex's favorite resting place in my absence was a patch of hallway floor just to the left of the door of my study. To reach the doorway, without stepping over him, one had to veer sharply to the right, making a detour of several feet from the direct line of march from hall to study.

Now here comes something, perhaps of no significance, but whose truth I can corroborate by fully a dozen people:

Bruce was a beautiful, great, dark-brown-and-white collie of whom I have written elsewhere. He was my chum. Always he lay on the study rug at my feet, while I was writing there. The study was his chosen abiding place when he was indoors.

From the day of Rex's death, Bruce would not set foot on the spot in the hallway where the crossbreed used to lie.

To avoid treading there, he would make a circling detour on entering or leaving the study.

It was precisely as though he were walking around some unseen creature lying where Rex had been wont to lie.

Time and again, I have tested this odd trait of Bruce's. More than once when some guest was at Sunnybank—Ray Long and Sinclair Lewis and Bob

Ritchie, among others—I would tell Bruce to go into the study, and I would ask the visitor to watch his erratic course.

Invariably, the collie would skirt widely that one tabooed spot, instead of traveling in a bee-line.

So much for my four facts. I refuse to draw an inference from any of them. I don't pretend to say whether or not any of them is significant.

They happened. That is all I can vouch for.

Add them up to suit yourself; or brand the whole lot of them as an uninteresting jumble of lies. Moreover, they can be explained, perhaps, on normal grounds. For instance:

It may be that Healy remembered how Rex had lain at my feet in other years; and that, by some throwback of memory, he imagined the crossbreed had been there on this particular evening.

Or, by the flickering firelight, he may have mistaken one of the collies for Rex. (Though I did not recall that any other dog had been indoors.) Either of these suppositions is quite within reason.

It may be that Grannis—the man who was drinking beer with me in the dining room—also mistook one of my long-haired collies for a larger and short-coated dog of somewhat different color, and with Rex's nose scar.

The sunlight may have been in the man's eyes. Possibly such a mistake could have been made.

It may also have been mere coincidence that he

chanced to describe a dog whose general appearance was like Rex's.

Bruce may have taken some wholly explainable dislike to treading on that one bit of hallway. He may at one time have slipped there, when the floor was new-oiled; or he may have picked up a pin or a tack there, in one of his feet.

Such a happening might have given him an aversion to that patch of flooring. The fact that Rex used to lie there may have had nothing at all to do with his avoidance of it. As for his skirting it because he was walking around an invisible ghostly animal—that idea is perhaps too absurd to touch on!

It does seem fitting, though, that the only ghost story I have to tell of Sunnybank should concern Rex, the crossbreed whose devotion to me in life was so extraordinary that everyone noticed it, and who died in disgrace after his battle with gallant old Lad.

Sitting here on the Sunnybank veranda in the twilight, Larry Trimble listened to the story I have just told you. Then, speaking half under his breath, he told me a companion tale to it. I asked him if I might use it some time. He said I might. So I am taking advantage of his leave.

Larry Trimble, by the way, was the first man to create a really great dog story for the screen. His hero was the grand police dog, Strongheart. And *Strongheart*, I think, was the name of Trimble's mightily successful picture.

(The screen is waiting for good dog stories—

though its magnates don't seem to know it—and Trimble was the first to scratch the surface of a bottomless vein of gold.)

Here is the yarn he told me:

"I was a kid, up on my father's farm. We had no dogs. I didn't know anything about dogs in those days and I was afraid of them all. My father was a just man, but he was stern. He worked hard and he expected everyone else on the farm to do the same. Especially me.

"One day I had been in the red-hot hayfield since dawn. I was tired out, in every inch of me. Early in the afternoon my father sent me back to the barn for some more water for the men.

"I ran fast, tired and hot as I was. For I figured I might steal five minutes of sleep in the haymow, before I went back to the field with the water jug. So I sneaked up into the barn loft and lay down on the hay for a snooze. In a second I was dead asleep.

"I was waked by my father shouting at me from the ground below. I jumped up and answered him and started to clamber down the ladder from the loft. It was then I saw that night had fallen. It was pitch dark, except for the lantern my dad carried.

"I had slept for five or six hours. That meant I hadn't carried the water to the men in the hayfield. It meant I hadn't milked the cows or done any of my other evening chores.

"My father was raging mad at me. As he heard me start down the ladder he opened a bombardment of scorching language. At the same time I saw him snatch up a wagon spoke. I knew I was in for the worst thrashing I had ever had—and that was saying a lot.

"I was only a little chap; and I was scared sick at what was before me. Somehow I forced myself to keep on going down the ladder toward him. But every step was torture. I've never been so frightened, before or since.

"Then, all at once, as I reached ground and as my father came stamping toward me with the wagon spoke swinging high in air, Something rough and shaggy pressed against my shaking palm. It was too dark for me to see anything. But I could tell by the feeling that it was an enormous dog.

"I wasn't afraid of him, somehow. I knew he was my protector. I grabbed his head with my hand and I yelled at Father:

" 'You don't dare hit me! You'll never dare lay hands on me again. If you do, HE will tear your throat out!'

"I can remember, even now, how Dad looked at me, there in the lanternlight. For perhaps a minute we faced each other. I wasn't scared any more. I knew my invisible dog would guard me. Then Dad turned on his heel and went back to the house. Never again did he strike me.

"Maybe he thought I was crazy from the heat. Maybe he thought he saw what I thought I felt. I don't know."

"Always after that, when I was in a bad jam, I could feel that shaggy head thrust itself into my hand. And I stopped being afraid. Because I knew I was safe from harm.

"A few years later I went to New York to look for a job. I was a country boy. I'd never been in the city, before. As I got to the corner of Broadway and Forty-second Street, I saw thousands of people who seemed to be bearing down on me. They were coming from every direction and they were pouring up out of the subway.

"I had a moment of panic. I wanted to run screaming away from them before they could tear me to pieces. Just then the great rough head pushed itself under my sweating and trembling palm. And I knew I was safe.

"Nothing could harm me while my invisible guardian dog was there close beside me. I stopped being afraid.

"Well, from then on, every time I was frightened, I could feel that phantom dog's presence at my side to shield me from danger. Long afterward, It vanished for good. I've never felt It near me again. It has gone forever. When do you suppose It went away?"

"When first you knew the love of woman," I replied, with no hesitation at all.

Trimble stared at me, perplexed.

"Oh," he muttered, "then I've told you the story before?"

"You didn't have to," I said. "I knew the answer. Yours isn't the first nor the thousandth case. They all end alike."

CHAPTER NINE

Car-sick

HERE is a story that IS true. It happened to Rusticus Smith, on a golden spring Sunday morning. To Rusticus Smith who lives only four miles from Sunnybank. And in varying degrees it happened to many thousands of other country dwellers, that spring day. Here it is:

Rusticus Smith and his pretty young wife stood on the porch of their house, after breakfast, looking happily about their small domain, sweet in the May sunshine.

Their gaze rested presently on the white tentlike branches of a beautiful young dogwood tree, at the gateway of their grounds. The warm weather had caused the lovely tree to blossom, overnight.

As they watched, a motor car tooled past the gates. It slackened speed and stopped. A woman in its rear seat was pointing delightedly to the shapely tree and its snowy blooms. The driver jumped to the ground. He ran back to the entrance to the grounds, and approached the dogwood.

Before the Rusticus Smiths could intervene or even

guess the man's intent, the motorist ripped seven or
eight of the brittle spreading branches from the tree;
tucked the flowery plunder under his arm, ran back
to the car, handed his armful of boughs to the woman
in the back seat, jumped to his seat and set the machine
in rapid motion.

(At dusk that evening, at the ferry, the woman
tossed the wilted and worthless armful of dogwood
out of the car window into the roadway. It was by
no means the only pitiful heap of murdered and discarded spring verdure-and-bloom—dogwood, mountain laurel, wild azalea—lying scattered along that
ferry road. Some of the shrubs or trees bloomed in
Sunnybank's own roadside woods—close to the turn-
pike.)

Twice, during the next hour, did Rusticus Smith
arrive at his despoiled dogwood tree just too late to
prevent further mutilation of its graceful boughs and
their snow-flowers.

He arrived just too late, incidentally, to save a score
of purple lilac clusters, hanging out over his hedge,
from being torn off, along with their branches, by a
motorist who drove so close to the hedge that he did
not even need to dismount from his car in order to
grab them.

At noon, when Rusticus returned to the porch from
writing a letter, he beheld a pleasingly rural picture in
the middle of his lawn.

Four motorists had parked their car in his driveway and had spread for themselves a picnic luncheon

on the close-cropped emerald grass. Already, swathes of eggshells and chicken bones and greasy paper and greasier wooden dishes adorned the lawn which Rusticus Smith had toiled so hard to make bright.

Two members of the party were lighting a camp fire, against the trunk of an ancient oak tree in the center of the lawn. For kindling, they were using Smith's "No Trespass" sign, and parts of a picturesquely ancient rustic bench which had stood just beneath the flame-stabbed oak.

"This is private property!" stormed Rusticus Smith, bearing down on the lunchers. "You are trespassing here. Get off at once! First put out that fire. It will ruin the tree. And clean up the filthy mess you've scattered all over the grass. Then clear out, or I'll have you arrested for trespass! I——"

He got no further. Apparently, Rusticus was an unconscious humorist; to judge from the cackle of amusement which drowned his indignant words. Three of the party laughed in high glee.

The fourth—a woman—alone remained mirthless. Flushing, she exclaimed in wrath:

"Nice way to speak to a lady, isn't it? Who do you think you are, anyhow? God's green earth don't ALL belong to you, does it?"

"This land belongs to me," returned Rusticus, "and it is posted. I must ask you to get off of it, please. It——"

"Hasn't the poor workingman got *any* rights?" spoke up one of her male companions, truculently.

"He's got to sweat and slave in the hot city all week, hasn't he? And then when he takes his family out for a little ride on Sundays, hasn't he got the right to sit down peaceful, somewheres, and eat his dinner? Tell me that! A lot of you high-hatters think you're the whole works, just because you've happened to buy a piece of cheap ground and a shack—most likely mortgaged for more'n it's worth. You think you can order decent people off, like they was dogs."

The "poor workingman's" hands were flabbily soft and white. His car was of a make at least $1,000 more expensive than Rusticus Smith's own. He and his family wore many and expensive clothes on this innocent little springtime outing of theirs into the heart of nature.

All this their involuntary host saw, even as he listened to the objurgations heaped on him.

Rusticus was a small man, deficient in physical strength and indeed a semi-invalid. He had bought this country home as an aid to regaining his ruined health. He was no match for either one of the oversized men of this party of four picnickers. Even had he been able to thrash them both, he would have been too sane to incur endless damage suits by doing so reckless a thing.

"I am going to call up the police," he said, with what calm he could muster; and he strode back toward the house.

Well did he know the dreary futility of his threat. There were but two policemen in that hinterland rural village. On a Sunday, both of these were certain to be on traffic duty at busy road-crossings. The nearest State Police barracks were fully twelve miles distant.

Rusticus was helpless. Worse than helpless. He knew it.

As he looked back over his shoulder, from the doorway of his house, he saw another picnic party turn into his grounds, attracted probably by the very apparent immunity of the first. These latecomers had a tonneauful of fading mountain laurel and dogwood; ravished from the roadside and from privately owned lands adjoining it.

This pointless story of Rusticus Smith is true. The motorists who overran Rusticus Smith's pretty little estate knew by long experience that they were playing safe. At worst, some local constable might be summoned to order them off the lawn. In that case, there were plenty of other lawns or groves or posted sylvan hillsides whither they could go. For breaking into a country estate and defiling its carefully tended grounds with lunch rubbish and for picking its flowers and shrubs and injuring its stately trees—there was no adequate penalty.

Yes, they played safe; even when Rusticus Smith's rolypoly chow puppy dashed across the driveway in pursuit of a squirrel, as their car rolled out.

They were going rapidly, because it looked like rain. They did not see the puppy. And, as they were all singing, they did not hear his scream of unbelieving horror and agony as the right front wheel left him writhing his life out in the gravel of his master's driveway.

Throughout all the smiling countryside, that May morning, for a thousand miles, the same kind of thing was happening to a thousand owners of country homes.

What is the answer? *I* don't know.

What is the remedy? Apparently there is none.

The city dweller is hedged in on every side by protection. The country landowner has not one right which the motor-tourist is forced to respect. This latter statement is sweepingly radical, I know. But it is 100 per cent accurate in every detail and ramification.

If the cry "Back To The Soil" and its kindred "Own Your Own Home" slogan are shouted more and more insistently, every year, perhaps some practical measure for the protection of the Back-To-The-Soiler may be worth framing. Up to now, there is none.

There is a kinsman of the vandal motorist, only a shade less objectionable than is the vandal himself. He is the car-owner who likes to vary his country rides by dropping into various strangers' homes on tours of inspection.

There are literally millions of him (far more often "him," by the way, than "her").

Here, for instance, is an inviting driveway, winding down through trees or shrubs toward an unseen house. True, there are "No Trespass" signs on either side of the gates. But what do those matter?

True, the signs say clearly that the owner of this place begs for the right to as much privacy as is accorded to the dweller in a tenement hall-bedroom. True, they say in effect:

"This is my home. It is also my one refuge from the outer world. Won't you strangers please keep out? You are not wanted here."

Yes, the signs say all that. But does that turn him back? No. The driveway is inviting. This estate may be worth seeing. Let's go on in, and see what we can see.

So in he goes. Perhaps the owner and his family are at lunch on the veranda. Perhaps they are strolling about their beautifully arranged grounds. Perhaps they are merely resting. Perhaps they have guests of their own inviting.

What difference does that make? None at all. Let's drive through the grounds, anyway. This is a free country, isn't it? Let's take a once-over and see how they live. Come on. Nobody'll hurt us. If we're stopped, we can say we're just looking around.

I wonder if there is any owner of a fairly attractive country home—whether the home be big or small—whose privacy has not been invaded, numberless times, in this way. Often the intruder will even honor his unknown hosts by stopping at the house and paying a sketchy volunteer call.

I am speaking, mind you, of country-places at large. Not merely those of the artist or the actor or the writer or the musician of more or less note who seeks the quiet and charm of the wilds and who thus becomes a sort of intellectual-or-curiosity filling station for motorists who pass his home.

Even the most obscure bushleague lionlet—myself, if you like—bids farewell to anything resembling privacy when the motor world learns the path to his door.

I have heard Edith Wharton criticized sharply for the sign "Keep Out! This Means YOU!" which is said to adorn the entrance to her New England home. To me, in view of all she must have had to bear from unknown motorists, the sign seems almost servile.

In my own far more humble sphere, my gate sign, "No Admittance Today," flanked by two "No Trespass" signs, has won me an endless mass of abuse— much of it in the form of anonymous letters. It might have gleaned far more unpopularity for me had the average passing motorist done me the honor to regard it at all. Usually, he drives in, heedless of the request.

Usually, too, he scoots down my winding furlong of private driveway at top speed, in spite of a series of big "Please Drive Slowly" signs which disfigure the trees en route.

It is due to this freeborn disregard of signs that my friendliest collie—little Sunnybank Jean—was crushed to death and disemboweled not long ago by some motorists from Detroit, and that another collie had her hip broken and was crippled for life, and that the foreleg of another was smashed, and that several kittens have been killed—all of them butchered blithely by self-invited strangers; to make a motor holiday. All of the victims were well within the confines of my own posted land.

Carleton Ford told me a tale he said Rudyard Kipling had told him. He said Kipling was hard at work in his study when the door was banged open. On the threshold stood a fat man in motor togs and a mealy-faced boy.

Silently, gogglingly, for a moment, the two intruders stared at the dumbfounded writer. Then the fat man announced:

"Son, *that* is Kipling!"

Turning, after another long stare, the two tramped out of the room and downstairs and out of the house, to their waiting car.

Yes, a throng of better known public or quasi-public characters than I am could tell a throng of infinitely more incredible tales of motor intrusion. Why prolong the roster? It is all the same general story of trespass and of unwarranted vulgarity.

The plea of five in ten of the Sunnybank motorist trespassers is that they have read some of my books or of my stories or essays. They seem to think this gives them plenary rights to overrun my home at all hours.

I don't get the logic of it. But the plea is so nearly universal that it must have some occult cogency. And I have yearned to be elsewhere than on the receiving end of the outrage.

We country dwellers pay stiff taxes to make our highroads broad and smooth and attractive for pleasure-seeking motorists. We open up costly new routes for them through the more picturesque regions.

There are public parking spaces, picnic grounds, lunchrooms, garages, golf courses, everywhere, for their free use and convenience; often to the detriment of the landscape.

In spite of all this, increasing hordes of them seem to find their truest life-happiness only in invading our homes. Those of them who don't dirty the grounds of these homes by their picnic rubbish and camp fires cannot resist the temptation to regard our lands as public highways and to make unasked and undesired visits to householders whose distaste to receive them is expressed unmistakably by the words, "NO TRESPASSING."

We tired and hard-worked folk move to the country for rest and for quiet and for a meed of privacy. If we wanted an army of motor-tourists to pour into our grounds, we would erect signs at our gates, reading:

"*PLEASE come in, Strangers!*"

But perhaps the same invitation is conveyed subtly in the "No Trespass" signs. At all events it is accepted.

Nearly two thousand years ago, a parable was spoken, about a landowner in rural Palestine who bade his servants:

"Go ye into the highways and the byways, and *compel* them to come in!"

If the landowner had lived some nineteen hundred years later, that famed command need never have been given. Instead, one can picture him saying miserably to his servants:

"Never mind replacing those torn-down 'No Trespass' signs. No motorist ever paid attention to them, anyhow. Irvin Cobb's goldfish was an invisible hermit, for privacy, compared to the poor guy who owns a place in the country."

The Mistress contradicted me, when I said something of the kind.

"You're mistaken," she told me. "The 'No Trespass' signs and the 'No Admittance' sign really *do* have some effect. They keep out all the friends we'd love to see, and they let in only the noisy swarm of strangers."

CHAPTER TEN

De Senectute

I wish I knew a good definition of the word "old."
It is all so comparative! There doesn't seem to be
any standard, any measuring rod. For instance:

Folk who have built homes hereabouts during the
past seventy years speak of Sunnybank House as old.
The few surviving owners of Pompton's colonial
homes speak of it as though it were all-but new.

I brag of Sunnybank oaks, whose age is proven by
pre-Revolutionary deeds to be fully two hundred and
forty years. But in California I have seen groves of
redwoods which science says were full grown when
the patriarch, Abraham, dwelt in Ur. Compared with
them my Sunnybank oaks and my largest ancient
elm are as blades of new-sprung grass.

Sunnybank House is in its late seventies, as regards
years. The California missions, some of them, date
back into the 1780's; making Sunnybank crudely
modern by contrast.

Cross to England, and you will find a thousand

houses and public buildings many centuries older than the oldest mission.

"From the west traveling east," stop off at Rome; where stand or crumble a host of edifices which were in mellow age before Great Britain could boast any structure more pretentious than a mud-and-wattle hut.

Then if you still care to travel east go a bit farther and note the buildings on the Acropolis; temples and the like that were the glory of Greece when Rome was a baby.

Another step and Egypt will show you pyramids and friezed tombs that were erected before the Hellenes made their first raid from the north and drove the primitive Pelasgians out of the hillside village which one day was to become Athens.

The age-seeking trip could be carried to lands whose structures antedate Cheops' Pyramid and the Luxor tombs by greater space of time than Rome's buildings antedate Britain's.

And so it goes. The whole thing is a question of comparison, of contrast. Perhaps, after all, nothing is basically old or basically young. For us aging men that is a mildly comforting thought.

Again, when Bob Fitzsimmons was thirty-seven years of age he begged me to write of him as "the Grand Old Man of the Prize Ring"—which he was. Abraham Lincoln in his late twenties was called "Old Abe."

In early 1918 the gray Hindenburg hosts smashed

their way through a British army. By way of excuse, military experts declared the commanding general of the broken army had been far too young to be placed in a position of such responsibility. The general was forty-seven years old.

Fitzsimmons was old at thirty-seven.

The British general was "too young" at forty-seven. Just what is age and just what is youth?

Most sprinters start downhill before they are twenty-five. Most brainworkers don't get into their best stride before they are forty.

All this dreary and bad-logic preamble to lead up to the wholly inconsequential tidings that I think I am growing old. And that I am trying to scrape together a lapful of consoling lies to assure me I am not.

I have not been old long enough to keep from talking about it. Not long enough to keep from resenting it as I might resent some scurvy joke played on me.

Age has not made me wise. But it has added yearly to my junk heap of experience and of observation until the blend of the two is beginning slowly to add up to something akin to a pseudo wisdom; something which is more interesting than useful to me.

"The dunce who's sent to Rome excels the dunce who's kept at home" only because he has seen a thousand more new sights, met a thousand more people, heard a thousand unfamiliar truths and lies spoken and had a thousand new viewpoints forced upon him.

Increasing age is the Rome to which I have been

sent. It has taught me much that the cleverest young homestayer does not know. I think that is how age wins its unearned repute for wisdom.

Not that the things I have discovered—most of them—are of the remotest value to me now. The evolving of an unhittable pitching delivery would not profit an elderly baseball player who is doubled up with chronic arthritis. Nor would a new-found knack of supreme marble-playing be an asset to an elderly banker. Get the idea?

The Spaniards are a wise people, except perhaps as concerns their own welfare. And the Spaniards long ago summed up what I have been groping to say, in their bitterly true proverb:

"God gives walnuts to those who no longer have teeth to crack them."

If one could always keep on feeling old, one would become resigned to the sorry state; as to a wooden leg or to a double set of false teeth. But one can't. At least, *this* one can't.

I am sixty-one. Possibly by the time I hobble past the eightieth milestone, I may have become used to the whole wretched thing and forget that once I was anything else. By then I may have acquired the foul mixture of exhaustion and bloodless apathy which folk miscall Philosophy.

That is something jolly to look forward to. Almost as much as is a half-grain shot of morphia to a peritonitis patient. It doesn't check the malady, but it stops the hurt.

Yet even eighty may have its sore moments. I know that from talks with two old ladies I used to go to see every now and then, out of a mistaken idea that my calls cheered them up.

One of them was eighty-six. She lived within walking distance of Sunnybank. I dropped in at her farm one afternoon and I found her sitting in a diseased old porch rocker, looking monstrous miserable. Her bleared gaze was trained on the roof of the nearby barn where a line of pigeons were perching on their cotes.

"I been watching them pesky doves," she hailed me gloomily. "They make me dretful sad. You see, I've got so, now, that I can't shin up onto the barn ridgepole any more, to hunt their nests for squabs. Leastwise I'm pretty sure I can't. I ain't tried, lately; 'count of me being chair-ridden."

"But why should you want to climb up there?" I asked her. "Isn't there anyone else to get the squabs for you?"

"Plenty of folks, I s'pose," she said. "But *I* can't. That's why I git to grieving when I look up there. It'd—it'd be kind of fun to——"

"How long ago was the last time you climbed to the ridgepole?" I asked. "Or can you remember?"

"I remember fine. I ought to. It kept me from going to a grand party Clark Mills's wife was giving that night. I shinned up there that morning and I slipped and fell onto a wheelbarrow down below and bust my left ankle. I was laid up with it for weeks.

No Clark Mills party for me then. Nor yet any other gay doings."

"But," I ventured, puzzled, as I dipped far back into childhood memories, "Clark Mills and his wife have been dead for nearly half a century. If——"

"Oh, this was years and years afore they died. I wasn't but only just barely sixteen."

Seventy years earlier! For seven decades, presumably, no thought of shinning up to the ridgepole had crossed her mind. Yet, at eighty-six, it was her bitterest grievance against life that she could not do so any more.

She was one of the two ancient dames of my acquaintance who still girded against the drawbacks of age. The other was barely eighty-one, and had borne twelve children. She was an ardent mother, a woman to whom motherhood was the crown of earthly and heavenly bliss.

One day when I called on her during a hike from Sunnybank I found her shedding the scant and difficult tears of old age. At sight of me she wiped her eyes in a shamed way and tried to talk vivaciously. When I sought to learn what she had been crying about, she was loath to speak of it. At last, defiantly, she blurted forth:

"My boys and girls have all grown up or died. I miss them so! And sometimes I get downright despondent when I realize there's a strong chance I may never have another child."

One octogenarian had mourned the loss of her squab-catching prowess. The other had mourned the possibility of future childlessness. Truly, extreme age insists sometimes of having its woes; no matter how far afield it may have to search for them.

But there is another side to the rare picture of non-resigned senescence.

I used to spend the twilight hour nearly every day with my mother when my own daily writing chores were done. One afternoon when I went to her home at dusk, I found her lying on a couch. She was eighty-nine. A few months later her blindness was to set in.

Almost never had I seen her lying down in the day-time. She seemed half-ashamed to be caught so, now. I asked if she were ill.

"No," she told me, getting up briskly. "But I have been at my desk for nine solid hours today. An editor wanted an article in a hurry. I finished it, a few minutes ago. And I feel just a little tired. You—you don't suppose that's a sign I'm beginning to grow old, do you?"

At seventy she had broken her right wrist. Always until then she had written by hand. She taught herself to compose on the typewriter. At ninety she went blind. Cheerily, she taught herself to dictate—a thing she never had done—and dictated a novel, *The Carringtons of High Hill*, which had a good and long-lived sale.

So you see when eighty-odd refuses to be eighty-odd, there is more than one one angle to its unrest.

If only age could hit us between the eyes in a single vigor-crushing swat, it would be so much easier to endure! One could face it then as one faces a sudden misfortune or an accident.

But the thing crawls up to its victim so gradually, so insidiously, that it has established permanent and ever-strengthening headquarters before its beastly presence is guessed at. And then what a set of pitiful lies we tell ourselves and others about the growing calamity!

The daily swinging ten-mile cross-country tramp is whittled down to a slower and shorter walk. Bit by bit this is done and with a running comment of explanation.

"I'm as young and as husky as I was twenty years ago. But I got a twinge of rheumatism from not changing my wet shoes. It hurts me when I walk too far or too fast. It'll be all right, presently. Besides, I figure my heart is a little out of kilter—just for the time. Because I start puffing and I feel queer inside and in my legs when I do any stiff mountain climbing. But I'll get back to it, soon. . . . No, I can't eat as hoggishly and get as much of a kick out of my meals as I did. But that's just because my system has trained itself at last to eat sanely. . . . I can't sit up till all hours, as I did. But that's because I'm getting more common sense. . . . My chest is slipping down and my waistline is changing to wasteline. But I'll get rid of that, fast enough, as soon as this rheumatism and heart let me take some man's size exercise again."

The pity of the babyish self-fooling! Yet we are sincere about it—at first. Everyone else sees we are aging, before we do. And it is one of life's genuinely black moments when at last we must give up lying to ourselves and face the sour, hideous truth.

Perhaps, after all, it is better that the disease creeps imperceptibly upon us instead of leaping upon us.

My father never would admit he was aging. This because he had not the remotest knowledge of it. When he was past seventy-six—a bare month before he died—I saw him breast the steepest and highest hill at Sunnybank, and stride up it with the ease and swiftness of a boy. At the top he was unbreathed and sweatless.

I could no more climb that hill at sixty-one with his athletic stride and lack of fatigue than I could run up the side of the Empire State Building. His own father took long horseback rides every day until he was ninety-three.

They bred *men* in those days. Men whom age was afraid to tackle until well on toward sunset.

I suppose every boy or girl yearns unspeakably to be a grown-up. I did. So did the children I knew. I had it all figured out, by the time I was ten years old. Some day there would be a loud click inside of me and perhaps a convulsive shiver. That would mean I was a man. No longer an unconsidered kid, but a man grown.

For half a century I have been waiting in vain for that click and shiver. I did not so much as know when I crossed the borderland into adulthood. I know only it was much earlier than anyone but myself could be lured into believing.

It was so when I entered middle age. It was so when I left sixty behind me. Something or other must have marked the several transitions. Or must it? Often I have wondered. I realized them only when they were a goodly—or a badly—distance behind me.

In novels I have read of experiences which "turned him overnight from a boy into a man" or turned a sturdily mature man into an oldster. In real life I have looked for such cases, with no success at all. I wonder if they exist, outside book covers. So many things don't!

It was a motor car's fifty-mile-an-hour slap, a few years ago, which taught me slowly that I was aging. During my months in bed and on crutches I began with gaping incredulity to learn the bleak lesson. And I asjusted myself as well as I could to the new life which the old must lead.

Mentally—such slight mentality as has been mine—I seemed as good as ever. I could write as long at a stretch and as semi-acceptably and as much. But physically I must slow down. And either I could grouch about it or I could make the best of it.

At any rate, I didn't lie to myself. Not to any great extent.

When the adjustment at last is made, there still is a lot of fun in life at sixty-odd. How much fun there may be at seventy or eighty, I don't know. And I don't like to look forward so far.

When those moldly ages arrive they may bring with them their own antiquated stores of good times;

though I'm blest if I can foresee what kinds of fun a septuagenarian or octogenarian can scare up.

But then, at fifty, I looked forward with the same sick foreboding to sixty. I wrote a book, eleven years ago, called *Now That I'm Fifty*. It was almost literature. In spots. One of those brochures everybody praises and nobody buys. In it I sought primly to reconcile my fellow-semicentenarians to their doddering state.

I glanced at the book, a little while ago. And with dull amazement I realized how little difference there may be between fifty and sixty. Both periods are embodied in the Indian summer of life.

Behind, of course, are left the high promise of spring and the fierce-glowing heat of summer. But the cold fogs of November and the deadly white chill of winter are still a fairish distance away. So far away that we needn't peer tremblingly forward at them. Sometimes.

A wiser man than I has written this definition of old age:

"A man is old when he keeps saying to himself: 'I'll feel as well as ever in a few days.' "

He won't feel as well as ever. But it is soothing for him to think he will. Age is an incurable disease which waxes worse every year. In a play a few seasons ago a woman asked her fifty-five-year-old husband if he was well. He made grumpy reply:

"*No* man over fifty is well!"

Yet there are compensations in fifty and in sixty, when one has slowed down but has not yet bogged down. I've noticed them, even if I haven't bothered to tabulate them all. For example:

People are much more courteous to me than when I was younger. Much less plain-spoken in argument. Many of them listen to my platitudes with greater semblance of interest than in the years when I was better worth listening to.

Naturally, my common sense tells me they are cursing me for a prosily garrulous old bore. But I can shut my mind to that knowledge. (As we grow older we are more and more content to accept things at their face value and not to dig too deep under the surface to where the ill-smelling truth crouches.)

Thus it is pleasant to receive kinder and more flattering treatment than of yore, from many of those about me. I grant it might be better-bred of me not to impose on such courtesy. But I am selfish—another emolument of age—and I enjoy being a pest to those who will permit it.

Then—if age has the moderate means for it (and age needs much less cash than does youth or middle age)—there is a genuine sense of luxury in allowing the pace to slow down. To take things easy. Not to rush, but to cultivate the beautiful art of laziness—an art which merges more and more into necessity as the years whiz past.

That occasional indolence is the best recipe I know for checking the speed of the aging process.

I know a great man, some ten years or twelve years

older than I am. A man who gets through a tremendous volume of brilliant work and who seems tireless. A few years ago, he went to pieces. Then he staged a gorgeous comeback. Through following the orders of a Vienna specialist.

The specialist gave commands to him which are worth pasting in the hat of any aging man or woman who can afford the time to obey them:

"As soon as you are able to take up the business of life again, this is the routine you must follow: Lie in bed late in the morning. When you get up, take your time in bathing and shaving and dressing and in eating your breakfast and reading your mail and the newspapers. Don't start work till between ten and eleven. Up till then, go easy. Loaf over everything you do.

"When you do get to work, you can hustle as hard as you want to, all day, till an hour or so before dinner. Then go home, undress and go to bed. Stay there for an hour, relaxed, dozing if you can. After that, get up and dress for dinner. When you've dined, go on working or attend any public function or do anything energetic that you want to. Go to bed for the night any time before one A.M."

In other words, the day must begin slowly and gradually and with no exertion of any kind. The afternoon must end with an hour of complete bodily and mental relaxation. Thus the system and the nerves are not flogged to the jar of sudden action, nor to the undue hurry which wears down more of us than does everything else.

The great man followed instructions. Not only did he get well, but he seems to have grown younger, more vigorous, more able to handle the vast amount of labor that is his during his daily work hours.

I crossed to Italy on the same leisurely boat with him not very long ago. He had just finished many months of toil. Acting on the same specialist's orders, he spent the first seventy-two hours of the voyage in bed; sleeping as much of the time as possible; not talking or even reading.

He came on deck at the end of the third day, wholly made over.

There is a catch somewhere in that phrase, "wholly made over." A bankrupt may seem wholly made over, financially, if a friend lends him a hundred dollars for current expenses. But the money goes fast, hoard as he may, and still he is bankrupt. An egg is as hard as marble—until it drops or until someone tries to break it. Old age's flashes of rejuvenation are wretchedly brief, at best; breeders of brutally false hope.

Did you see Philip Merivale—a gorgeous actor—in a rather tremendous play called *Death Takes A Holiday*? In it Death gives himself a three-day vacation from his lethal job. Consequently nothing and nobody withers or dies or feels the oncoming of dissolution during those three days.

One of the play's characters, a feeble old diplomat, braces up and wears a gardenia in his buttonhole and flirts ponderously and is overjoyed at his miraculous return of vitality. When Death's holiday is ended and the age-old process of decay is resumed, the diplomat whimpers:

"I thought I was growing young again. But I had only stopped dying!"

The occasional youthful flashes—the brief return of strength and spirits which God gives to the aging— they are only flowers sent to a sick-bed. For a day they make the grisly room cheerful. Then they wilt.

We are not renewing our youth. We have "only stopped dying." Why not be grateful for these short hours of surcease; not foolishly hopeful when they visit us nor grouchy when they depart? We'll get more fun out of them that way and no bad aftertaste.

The more we spare ourselves needless labor and needless speed and worry—the more sanely we treat these degenerating bodies and nerves of ours, the longer we shall last and the oftener will come the days of golden mirage.

Typhoid or pneumonia patients, in the last stages, are drugged by fever or by septic stupor. They feel little. They care less. They drowse to death. God grant it may be so with us who are fated to overlong lives! That day by day we may feel and care less and less. That we may fall asleep happily, heedless whether the doze is to endure forever or if there is to be an awakening. There are worse things for the tired than endless and dreamless rest. ("For so He giveth His beloved Sleep!")

From our ancestors has come down the fetish that it is shameful not to keep hustling all the time. That is well enough for young people who still have years of energy and supervitality stored up within them. But the man past fifty who tries to hit the same crazy pace is fraying a rope that never can be woven anew.

I have noticed too often and too unhappily the wise way our Sunnybank dogs take the slow onset of age. Dogs have been taking it the same way since countless centuries before the first Viennese specialist was born.

They adjust themselves by instinct to the ever-increasing let-down from swirling vitality to obese or emaciated senility. Something seems to whisper to them when to begin taking less and less violent exercise and to take longer and longer naps during the day and to spare themselves all needless effort.

The Sunnybank back porch at one end is a little more than two feet high from the ground. Some yards from this end are the steps, three or four of them, low and wide and easy. This porch is a gauge whereby I can tell the first active approach of old age in any of my collies.

When I go out on the back porch from the house, any of the dogs that are in sight come running to greet me. They take the sheer side of the veranda in their stride with no semblance of effort.

Then comes a day when one of them avoids the easy jump and trots along the walk on stiffening legs until he reaches the low flight of steps. He pads up these and thence trots along the porch toward me. He has gone many yards out of his way, sooner than to jump. And I know he is aging. I know it as well as he does.

It is only a span of time, then, until I catch sometimes the sharply pathetic "*old* dog look" in the eyes he lifts to mine. At first the look is momentary and it appears seldom. But in time it is permanent.

And by that time he will not climb the flight of stairs to the second story of the house unless he is summoned. Also he is spending the bulk of his spare hours in sleeping.

He knows how to take care of himself and how to save every savable atom of his fast-ebbing energy. Always except when the Mistress or I start out on a walk.

Then, no matter what the effort or how hot or cold or wet the day, the gallant oldster is on his feet; gaily eager to go along. And when kindness makes us shut him in the house or in a kennel-yard, to save him the fatigue of the hike he used to find so easy, he mopes morosely and his age-sharpened feelings are cruelly hurt.

Especially so was it with old Sunnybank Lad as age and weight began to encompass him. He had a mystic way of knowing when we were going for a walk. Wherever he might be lying, he would lumber heavily after us; straining every ancient muscle to catch up with us.

I don't know how many times we turned back to the house, abandoning our hike, when we saw the toiling mahogany shape heaving its tired way up the drive in our wake—Lad, who once had been the swiftest and strongest of all our collies.

I grant it was silly of us to abandon a bracing walk for the sake of humoring a pastworthy collie chum who loved us. But my own uncertain temper never went bad at such times. There would be chances for a thousand long walks after Laddie should be gone.

Of late years, when younger people have gone far out of their way to be nice to my aging self and to ease down their speed to mine, the picture has risen unbidden to my memory of our turning back from our walks to salve Laddie's feelings.

Perhaps the same principle obtains. Perhaps I am repaid in kind for my decency toward the outworn old Sunnybank collie. Who knows?

CHAPTER ELEVEN

Our Ramapo Wild Dogs

Two or three years ago a dog hunt was organized on the slopes of the Ramapo Hills beyond our lake and to the north of Sunnybank. So far as I know, neither it not its several predecessors rated mention in any press dispatch.

Yet there was a queer element to that hunt—one which was missing or unrecorded in the later and more widely advertised dog battues of the region.

Here is the tale, in brief:

A posse of clever local trackers banded together and fared forth against the predatory brutes. Almost at once they caught sight of several of the wild dogs slinking in single file among a scatter of hillside rocks, well out of shotgun range.

The trackers gave chase, using as much wile as speed. Some of these men were skilled deer stalkers. The job looked easy enough. The dogs did not seem to have made any special effort to confuse their trail. For many miles the quest continued.

But not another glimpse of the prey did the hunters get. At last, tired and discouraged, they turned back, heading for home.

It was then they found what had happened. The dogs had doubled, getting behind their trackers with no difficulty at all. Then they had followed the men—every step of the rest of the hunt.

Whether as a joke or out of curiosity, the dogs had trailed their hunters for perhaps six miles, sometimes traveling almost at the trackers' very heels, yet in such furtive silence that their presence never was suspected.

When the disheartened men turned back from their long hillside tramp the dogs melted into the thickets, leaving only that very distinct multiple track to show the trailers had been trailed.

Neighborhood newspapers in Pompton Lakes and Butler told the tale, but I don't remember that the press associations got hold of it.

It was nearly a half century ago that I had my first view of the Ramapo wild dogs. I was shooting partridges with my father in one of the more inaccessible folds of the hills. Five huge gaunt blackish dogs came in sight on the ridge just above us.

For perhaps a minute they stood there, outlined against the gray November sky. Then—well, the best way I can describe their departure is to say they weren't there any more. They didn't scurry out of sight. They simply *were not*.

My father looked worried. If the wild dogs were beginning to herd together as early as mid-November a hard winter was coming—a winter when hunger was due to send marauding packs of the savage brutes up and down the valley farms to wreak wholesale slaughter on livestock.

As usual, my father was right. That winter the dog pack took terrific toll of lambfold and cattle byre and hencoop, tearing to pieces the farm dogs that strove heroically to guard the stock of their masters.

Yes, and that winter the call went forth among the valley folk for a campaign of destruction against the marauding pests. Farmers by the dozen hunted them back into the hill fastnesses, shooting them right and left and cutting down their numbers so successfully that years went by before the raiders were plentiful enough and strong enough for general descent upon the valley.

Much nonsense has been written about the origin and the nature of these wild dogs of the Ramapos. I am going to waste a handful of words in setting down the truth—so far as anyone can know—about them.

Far back among that beautiful double swathe of mountains which is split in two by the rich Ramapo Valley and the Ramapo River dwell an unbelievably primitive race known as the Jackson Whites. Their forefathers fled to the hills to avoid work or to avoid the law, or both, long before the American Revolution.

Less than thirty miles from Manhattan Island as the crow is supposed to fly, many of them still live—or did live at last accounts that reached me—as lawlessly primitive a life as does any legendary Kentucky hill-billy.

They eke out their wretched means of livelihood in devious ways. They retain—or retained throughout the years of my own hunting trips through their hills—words and customs that date straight back to Eliza-bethan England.

For example, many of them still speak of "houses" as "housen" and give the Elizabethan suffix to a score of other words.

They follow the ancient custom of tying a shred of black cloth to the beehives of any of their number who has just died, and of pronouncing the dead man's name above each hive. That is an early English habit, as you may have read. But how or where did the Jackson Whites acquire these customs and these Elizabethan suffixes?

At dusk, when I was an undergraduate, I was coming down a Ramapo trail after a day's shooting. Up the trail toward me advanced a Jackson White. He was exceeding drunk and in a condition wherein the width of the trail seemed to bother him more than its length. At the top of his leathern lungs he was singing over and over again a couplet which ran:

> *If life was a thing that money could buy*
> *The rich would live and the poor would die.*

You will find that couplet, word for word, in a ribald book which deals with Skelton and his times—Skelton, as I recall, having been a poet in the reign of King Henry VII of England.

This description of the Jackson Whites and their ways is to explain their wild dogs. Almost every hovel of theirs used to be a harbor for one or more lanky curs. In my young manhood most of these lank dogs were black or blackish, and were as rangy as timber wolves. Indeed, their forebears had mated again and again with the wolves which long ago roamed those hills.

The average Jackson White was seldom more than a jump ahead of hunger. When a bad winter or some worse misfortune overtook him his first economy was to turn his starveling cur loose to shift for itself. The deserted animals banded into packs, led by the fiercest and craftiest and most wolflike of their number.

When there were enough of them to make the foray moderately safe, or when starvation crazed them, they descended on the Valley. More than once, it is reported, they attacked some wandering hunter or trapper in the hills and treed him. Woe to him if he could not get to a tree in time—or if his gun missed fire!

Of late years the strong breed characteristics of the wild dogs have changed. And this is easily explained. Farm dogs now and then "go bad." Some of these launch out on an independent career as killers. Others join the wild dog horde.

If these recruits are not at once ripped to fragments and devoured by the pack, they achieve full membership. In other words, the survivor is too formidable or too crafty to be killed. Thus he is in line to become a power in the pack and to blend his superior breed traits and brain power with it.

Still more recently there have been masses of recruits of a very different and lesser kind which will end by weakening the original stanch strain. For instance:

The banks of the Ramapo River are filling fast with bungalows. So is much of the once sweet solitude of the hinterland. Hordes of these casual summer visitors bring with them puppies or grown dogs of every grade from Pekinese to Great Dane.

When they go back to town in September they sometimes desert their canine pals. If it is a lush season, when famine does not scourge the wild dogs, some of these strays are permitted to join the pack unmolested. So are wretched dogs that have been dropped from motor cars along the highway.

All this has had a bad effect on the strength and prowess of the original pack. A melting pot is established whose residuum is something smaller and weaker and less wolf-like than was the original.

Of course, in hungry times the stronger can devour the weaker and thus do something to retain the old quality of the strain. But the change is certain and none too slow. In another decade or so at this rate the wild dogs of the Ramapo may inspire no more fear than would the mixed rabble found in a dog pound.

The New York *Herald Tribune* last year called attention editorially to the strange fact that the wild dog is found nowhere in the eastern states except in the Ramapos. I can't explain this. But I do know he is found—or was, a few years ago—in the sheep country in Tehama and Trinity counties in California.

There the valley stretches wide between giant mountain ranges. There, too, flocks of sheep numbering high into the thousands graze in unfenced pastures.

(There, too, in my day, worked the cleverest little black sheep dog I have seen either in America or in Scotland—a collie answering to the asounding name of Erastus.)

Out there, farm dogs and strays banded together and took to the mountains. From these fastnesses they avalanched into the valley from time to time, murdering sheep wholesale.

They were led by a giant black dog which was not only poison wise, but trap wise as well. Superstitious ranchmen vowed he bore a charmed life, and that he was more demon than dog. The pack obeyed him slavishly.

As a result of these wild marauders' killings, word was sent forth that any and every dog seen in a certain section of the valley was to be shot. The command was:

"Shoot first; then explain."

One of the first victims of the edict was a large and gentle house dog whose job in life was to draw his hopelessly crippled baby master in a cart. In Red Bluff, where the little cripple lived, there was hot resentment over this cruel slaughter. But the ranchers held grimly to their rule. Their flocks of sheep were their livelihood.

From time to time there have been doubts expressed

as to the actual existence of wild dogs in the East. On the suggestion of the *Herald Tribune* a committee of naturalists was sent to the Ramapos last year to verify or discredit the tales. On the strength of overwhelming testimony it verified them.

Many of the dogs turned loose by the Jackson Whites never returned to their owners' shacks, but went wholly wild, digging dens for themselves in the earth or preëmpting the stone caves of foxes.

There they reared their mongrel broods, feeding the pups and themselves on such small game as they could stalk or by organizing wolf-like hunts for deer when it was not safe or convenient to raid hencoops and folds and barnyards in the Valley.

I should like to tell you a rather unusual story of one of these original wild dogs. A story which may sound like a lie, but which was proved true in every detail. It happened while I was a half-grown boy. Its climax was seen by seven of my friends, including two relatives of mine. Here goes:

A likeable, lonely little foreigner moved to a half-sized farm not very far from Sunnybank. I am going to call him Schwartz, which was not his name. One day when he was hunting rabbits in the nearer Ramapos he heard a muffled whimpering.

Behind a windfall, sheltered by a ledge of rock, he found a grayish black puppy, perhaps a month old. There had been a periodical round-up and battue of the wild dogs. Probably this youngster's dam was among the slain.

Schwartz picked up the whining and squirming and

starving atom of puppyhood and got a needleprick bite in the thumb for his pains.

This very unpuppylike fierceness amused the man. He carried the waif home in a pocket of his shooting coat. There he proceeded to tame and bring it up. He named the youngster "Thor."

For the next few years the tamed wild dog and the lonesome little foreigner were inseparable pals. Never have I seen more complete devotion between master and dog.

Thor grew into a gigantic and rangy creature. His coat was the color of iron. He was an inspired farm worker, too, and a splendid guard and companion. He seemed wholly to have lost the wild strain, except that he would make friends with nobody except his master.

Then through the Valley ran the oft-heard sinister rumor that a killer was at large.

Fifty-one chickens were found killed—uneaten—in a nearby hencoop one morning. Forty white leghorn pullets suffered a like fate in a barnyard in the other end of the township. Thirty-seven Sunnybank chickens were slaughtered.

Eleven lambs, far up the Valley, had their throats and kidneys torn out. So did three yearling calves in still another neighborhood.

These were but a few of the killer's senseless murders. I say "senseless" because he never ate his kill. His entire joy was in the slaughter itself.

Early one morning a man came to Schwartz's home with a story of having rigged up a patent block-and-fall attachment on his hencoop door and of having re-inforced the coop's strength in divers other ways. That morning he had gone to see what luck he had had with his trap.

All of his fowls lay on the floor, their heads neatly bitten off. Up and down the coop, raging like a caged wolf, was—Thor.

The wontedly peaceful Schwartz flew into a fury. He knocked his informant down and filled the air with hot denials that his splendid chum was guilty. He ended by going with the man to the coop trap.

There stood Thor, his jaws bloody.

Schwartz broke down and wept. At sight of his master Thor shivered from head to foot as if with palsy. Head and tail adroop, he crawled to the little foreigner's feet and crouched there shuddering.

The farmer opened the coop door. Thor crawled out, trying pitifully to thrust his nose into Schwartz's palm. His master jerked his hand back in horror and said huskily:

"Go home!"

Thor cringed out of sight, looking wistfully back over his shoulders as he went as if for some sign of pardon. But no such sign was given him. Schwartz seemed in a drunken daze. Turning to the farmer, he muttered:

"Send me a bill for the chickens. I will pay it. And now I am going to Paterson to find a lawyer, to see if he can do anything to—to save my—my friend from death."

Schwartz hurried home and changed his clothes. As he moved around the house Thor followed him everywhere, begging mutely for a kind word or look. Schwartz paid no heed to him except to say as he started for the station:

"Keep where you are. Don't follow."

For once the giant dog did not obey his master's command. Skulking far behind Schwartz, he followed him to the station. A group of commuters and idlers were on the platform. Schwartz stood apart from them all, the picture of hopeless misery.

The train rounded the curve and came thundering toward the station. As Schwartz stepped forward a cold muzzle was thrust timidly into his cupped hand.

Schwartz glared at the miserable dog. Then he struck Thor across the head with his open palm. In all their happy years together the man never before had hit his chum.

Thor straightened up proudly, all sign of pleading gone from his manner. For a long instant he stared up into his master's face. Then with cold deliberation he stepped out in front of the oncoming locomotive.

The driving wheel of the engine cut him clean in two. With a roar, he lifted his forequarters and bit savagely at it. Then he was dead.

One wild dog of the Ramapos had paid his bill in the only way he knew how to pay it.

CHAPTER TWELVE

"The Rude Fourflushers of the Hamlet"

NOWADAYS the folk hereabout are much the same as everywhere else. The machine age extends to humans as well as to factories. But in my childhood, and earlier, this Pompton region of ours swarmed with odd characters and with their odder happenings.

As some of these people's descendants—painfully civilized and correct and modern—still live, I shall leave out nearly all names in touching on the high spots of their careers and themselves.

There was the man who, in the 1860's, lived in a funny little two-room stone house of colonial date. He raised ducks for a living. One day, he cut off the head of a duck destined for the Paterson market. The head bounded gorily into the lap of his nervous wife who sat close by. She fainted.

A few months later, her child was born. It was born with a head shaped in some fashion like a duck's; and with lips and nose hideously akin to a duck's bill. The

171

doctor carried the newborn infant out into the second room and showed it wordlessly to the father.

The man burst into a wild weeping; unheard by his wife who still was unconscious. He bade the doctor get rid of the monstrosity before the senseless woman should learn what it was.

Like nearly everyone else around here, the doctor looked on my father as a kind of confessor. Next day he came to Sunnybank and told his tale.

"I prayed for guidance, Dominie," he said, as he finished. "Then very gently I closed my fingers around that awful duck bill. I held them there till breathing stopped. Then the father and I buried It in the back yard, and we told the mother it had been born dead. What is your sentence on me for that?"

My father sat for a moment in thought. Then, solemnly, he made answer:

"I absolve you. You did right."

There was another event which since has been told a dozen times in verse and in story, vastly idealized. Up in the hills, across the lake from Sunnybank and on the edge of the Jackson White country, dwelt a Jackson White woman who had formed an alliance with a man from the Valley.

She had a grown son, from a former union. The man had two little children, a boy and a girl, by his newly-dead wife. The woman found these children a nuisance. So she went into executive session with her son.

The son took the children out on a nutting trip, one

bitter afternoon in early winter. He came home at dusk without them, telling their father they had "run off somewheres" and he couldn't find them.

Instantly the hunt was up. The hills were fine-combed for the lost boy and girl. They could not be found. The papers were full of the story.

A Paterson man read one of the printed accounts, just before he went to bed. Next morning he told his family and some neighbors and a newspaper editor about a strangely real dream that had visited him three separate times between sleep and waking. He said he dreamed he had joined in the hunt and had seen on a hilltop a dead tree shaped roughly like a cross—it still stood there in my own youth—and as he neared it an eagle flew from its summit and a wildcat slunk off among the rocks. At the foot lay the lost children.

The dream impressed him so strongly that he went to Pompton that same morning. He never had been in that part of the country before, but at once he saw and recognized the cross-shaped tree on the hill's crest. He made for it, climbing high and hard. An eagle flew from the treetop as he approached, and a wildcat crept into a cleft in the rocks.

At the base of the tree were the two children, frozen to death. The boy had pulled off all his upper clothes and had covered his little sister with them.

The story was spread far and wide, in a saccharine form. Money gifts came pouring in from everywhere to the stricken family. Then the Pompton neighbors took a hand in the game.

A deputation of them went to see the couple, and demanded they marry and that the woman's son be shipped out of the state before night. The orders were couched in terms which could not be disobeyed.

You may have read the tale, in a schoolbook or in other form. It used to be popular. But this is the first time a true version has been printed.

Then there was the patroon's family. They sat in a big square pew in the Pompton Reformed Church, just to the left of the pulpit. They jingled up to the door in a four-mule chariot driven by a black in faded livery.

When they entered the church the congregation rose and remained standing until the whole family was seated. This custom had antedated the Revolution by a century.

The pew was there when I was young, although the ancient rite recently had been abated. The last member of the family was very old when I was still a child. But I recall his bragging loudly—and somewhat boozily—to my father, in my hearing:

"As long as grass shall grow and water run, my name shall not pass from the memory of this village."

I doubt if anyone in the Pompton region, besides myself, so much as remembers the name today.

Then there was a night in my boyhood when every dog within a radius of three miles sat outside its kennel and made the air reëcho with a series of wild death howls.

(Have you heard a dog's death howl? Three times I have heard it. The last time was in June of 1922 when someone very dear to us died—died thirty miles away from my Sunnybank dogs. It is like no other sound on earth and it is not to be forgotten.)

At dawn, next morning, we found the body of a girl who had waded out waist deep into the half-frozen lake and had forced her head under water and kept it there until her pitiful life-story was ended.

The sorry game had had more angles to it than she could understand or endure. She had tired of it and she had sought this pathetic way out. But how did dogs, three miles away, know of that; and how and why had they swelled the chorus of the nightlong death howl?

Two days earlier the girl's father had stamped into her room, a shotgun under his arm. He had pointed to a newborn baby on the pillow beside her and had bellowed in black fury:

"Whose child is that?"

The unwed mother had roused herself from a daze and had answered gallantly:

"It is *mine!*"

Hell broke loose. At the end of forty-eight hours of it, the girl had stolen out of bed, kissed her sleeping baby on the mouth and laid on his breast her crucifix. Then she had staggered barefoot across the frozen fields to where the lake's ice-edged waters promised slumber to her.

The child is a slowly graying man now. Long ago

he left Pompton. Before he left he said to me with grim cynicism:

"In these up-to-date days Mother's escapade would have passed for a bit of sex repartee. What a pity she had to live in an age when such things were so serious they called for suicide or for a lifetime of glum Magdalene repentance! If only she could have lived when the motor car was an institution and when the concrete highway past your Place and casual European tours made such failings as hers not only possible but pardonable!"

There was an oldster who lived near Oakland, three miles from us; an Irish-born North Jerseyman who had fought from April, 1861, to April, 1865, in the Civil War. At Appomattox he had lost an arm, up to the elbow.

At his request, a murderous steel hook had replaced the amputated hand. This hook he learned to handle with incredible ease.

But, so ran local rumor, he did not learn soon enough. Seized by a sudden imperative itching he followed his instinct to scratch right vehemently; inflicting irreparable damage on himself.

But in my youth he could wield the hook as though it were a sentient hand. He became a dead shot and a peerless fisherman.

He shot his way through a circle of lively rattlesnakes on Rotten Pond Mountain, near the Jackson White district. At "still fishing" he had no equal.

He used to scull at high speed across the lake until he found by instinct the best spot for such fishing. Then he would bait and toss forth six lines.

I remember one morning my mother hailed him from the bank and offered him ten cents a pound for all the fish he might catch that day. At sunset he bore to our kitchen door no fewer than forty-seven pounds of bass and pickerel and perch.

My mother paid, like the square-shooter she was. We and our few neighbors had lake fish at our meals throughout the next week.

He wore his blue uniform to all local Grand Army picnics. These were half-yearly, in the mid-'eighties. A friend of his, a fellow veteran and fellow Irishman, was his boon companion at the rallies.

This friend's only drink at such celebrations was sarsaparilla, laced with Jamaica ginger. He would punish fully fifteen bottles of that ghastly mixture.

After which, while the one-armed man swung his lethal hook for silence, the sarsaparilla toper would chant stridently an endless song of which I recall only one quatrain:

Phil Sheridan was an Irishman born on American soil.
He won his way to em-i-nence through industry and toil.
He proved himself a hero bold at the Battle of Winchester.
Another Irishman who rose, his name was Daniel Webster.

His comrade's terrible hook protected the singer from interruptions, until the last of the many stanzas was droned forth. I found an awed joy in listening to his chant. Most of his adult hearers scowled and fidgeted. I wish I could remember the rest of the song. All of it was quite as good, or bad, as the verse I have quoted.

Then, in my childhood, there was a gentle little woman near Sunnybank whom my mother liked so much. Her grandfather's stables caught fire one night. The blaze was so hot the firemen dared not enter the doomed building. Instead, they poured water over a house some hundred feet away.

The timid little lady strolled calmly into the blazing stables, her arms laden with short blankets. She led forth to safety one blanket-blinded horse after another, until every one of the seven snorting brutes was rescued.

Always thereafter when I met her on the road I snatched off my cap, and I remained uncovered until she had trotted past me. A gallant deed wrought by a gallant woman! She is dead, long ago. Peace to her soul!

A penniless fortune hunter wooed and wed the plain daughter of the richest family within five miles of Sunnybank. Soon thereafter the bride realized what a fool she had been. Her infatuation turned to hate. One day the bridegroom came home from a trip to far-off New York. He brought her a two-thousand-dollar India shawl he had bought at A. T. Stewart's.

For a moment she eyed the rich gift. Then she

shouted to her Negro maid to fetch her soap and a pail of water. Plunging the two-thousand-dollar garment deep into the foaming pail, she dropped onto her knees and began to swab with it the dirty stone walk leading to the gate. Her husband cried aloud in horror.

"This is how I treat things you throw my fortune away on without my leave," she explained, still scrubbing. "That shawl was bought with *my* money!"

"Yes, by God!" roared her husband. "And so was *I!*"

A neighbor of ours—a breeder of fine horses—whom I knew fifty years ago, had a horror of thunderstorms. He was riding a spirited mare homeward one day when a black storm came up. He ripped a branch from a willow tree he passed under. With it he flogged the mare so brutally and to such speed that she dropped dead as she reached the stables.

The rider thrust the willow branch into the soaked ground and stamped indoors. The bough took root and grew into a tall tree; as often is the way with chance-planted weeping willows.

Twenty-one years later, mounted on a great-grandson of the killed mare, the man made another dash for home just in front of a gale-driven thunderstorm. As he rode beneath the willow, the wind uprooted it and the tree fell on him. His horse sped past unhurt. The rider's skull was crushed.

Back in my grandsire's time, long before my parents bought and built Sunnybank, two former Revolutionary officers, living near Pompton, quarreled. On the shady trail—where now the state highway runs—they met by chance. Each reached into a blue coat-tail pocket and flashed forth a pistol.

Both pulled trigger at the same time. One shot spat forth, scoring a clean miss. The other man's pistol would not explode. There was a stoppage somewhere in the narrow duct which led from the percussion cap to the powder.

Slowly and with infinite precision the defective pistol's wielder searched in his coat lapel until he found a pin. With this he cleaned out the clogged vent —his opponent meantime reopening fire with a second pistol—and leveled his cleansed weapon at the other man, pulling trigger afresh and drilling him through the knee-cap.

The mail was carried to and from the railroad station on foot, some two miles each way, by a thick-set little man with Uncle Sam gray chin whiskers. His name was Smith.

Because he made the bulk of his scant livelihood by breeding gamecocks and by fighting them illicitly, he was known as Chicken Smith. That was about all anyone knew about him. Nobody knew or cared whence he had come to Pompton, nor what his past life had been. He had lived there many years in a ramshackle yellow cottage on the river bank.

Apart from the tiny sum he drew from the government as mail toter and the larger amount from his gamecocks, his income was swelled by acting as guide to hunting parties from nearby towns and occasionally by bits of crude veterinary work.

For the rest he was insignificant, spoke with even greater illiteracy than did the general store's idlers, and was in every way the backwoods rube.

I had conditions in Latin and in Greek to make up during the summer before I went into college. One day I was sitting in the woods, studying, when Chicken Smith slouched through the underbrush with a hound pup he was teaching to course rabbits.

The little man's breath was aromatic with booze. It was the only time I had seen him in the least drunk, although there were tales of his historic sprees.

He stopped to chat with me. As we talked he took from my hand the copy of Anthon's *Lexicon*. He glanced at this, with muzzy interest. Then at the copy of the *Odyssey*.

He opened the latter book at random. Half under his breath, he began to read. He did not read as might a partly educated yokel nor even like an undergraduate; but as if he knew and loved it all.

For perhaps twenty lines he intoned the sonorous hexameters, while I stood open-mouthed. Next he translated with entire fluency what he had read. Before I could break the spell by babbling, his glance shifted back to the lexicon.

"Good old Doctor Anthon!" he mumbled, chuckling

in reminiscence. "Many a time and oft did he give me a whacking with that brassbound ruler of his. He could forgive any sin except ignorance of Greek."

Then Chicken Smith seemed to note for the first time that I was standing beside him. Over his face fell its wonted doltish aspect, changing it in a trice from a scholar's to a bumpkin's. He thrust both books at me, saying:

"Hey, sonny, take these here durn things. I never did set no store by l'arnin'. No good never come from it. Me, now, I can't read a word of 'em. What furren tongue might they be writ in? Eyetalian, maybe?"

He lumbered off through the woods, swearing at his hound pup.

Several years later there was a burglary epidemic in the neighborhood. Someone whose work seemed too clever to be mere local talent was making a careful round of the larger houses and using much discernment in the loot he took or discarded.

An informal posse was formed. It was led and directed by Chicken Smith. The thief was not caught. The posse chose always the wrong night for watching the wrong house. Betweenwhiles, other homes were plundered in entire safety.

That autumn Chicken Smith died from pneumonia after an illness of less than a week. His cottage was sold. Part of it was demolished to make way for a new wing.

The wreckers blundered upon a complete modern burglar kit, behind a sliding board between inner and outer wall. Also they found several things which had been stolen during the series of local burglaries.

That was all. Nobody knew more—nor knows more to this day—of little Chicken Smith.

Dr. Charles Anthon, of course, was America's foremost classical scholar up to his death in 1867. He was professor of Greek at Columbia; and he ran an exclusive private school in New York. But where in all that scheme did illiterate Chicken Smith fit in?

I have used Smith's real name—or Pompton name —in telling his story, because the account of the burglars' tools and of his suspected connection with the several robberies was printed in two or three newspapers soon after he died. And because he left no descendants.

Two brothers owned adjoining farms, across the lake from Sunnybank. My father said he never had seen brethren more deeply devoted to each other, for the first thirty-odd years of their lives. Then they quarreled.

Nobody—not even their wives—knew what the quarrel was about. But thenceforth the brothers were bitter enemies. They forbade their respective families to associate with one another.

One of them even transferred his membership to a more distant church, so that he need not sit in the same house of worship with his foe.

For a quarter century the hate endured. Then the elder brother fell desperately ill. Urged thereto by his wife and by his pastor, he sent his estranged brother a message saying that he was about to die and wished the quarrel might be made up.

The younger brother stalked into the sick man's home, the first time in twenty-five years that he had deigned to set foot on the premises; and was led to the death chamber. Loweringly he stared down at the gaunt occupant of the bed. Then he spoke.

"I'm sorry you weren't more of a man than to send that sniveling message to me," he growled. "But, since you did, I'm here to meet you halfway: If you die, I'll forgive you and I'll let bygones be bygones. But if you live, *the old grudge stands!*"

I heard my parents discussing in angry horror this death-bed speech. And, being a child, I had not the courage to turn their indignation against my callow self by saying it seemed to me rather tremendous. In any event, it would have fitted better into the *Heimskringla* than into a nineteenth century chronicle of Pompton, New Jersey.

Large families were the rule in this part of New Jersey in the dead days. The natives lived up to the Biblical command, "Increase and multiply," more strictly than to any other mandate of Holy Writ. Indeed, some of them could not have been more zealous if they had walked the earth in the age when Noah and his family had the whole job of repopulating it.

One of the larger families just outside of Pompton

contained eight sons and I don't know how many daughters. The sire was a man with a pleasing sense of humor and a pretty wit, as you shall see. His plump wife was a true Mother in Israel, and the soul of charity. But she could not read. Somehow she just never had got around to learning the trick of it.

Yet she had mighty reverence for the printed word and a childlike faith in its truth. She would sit in amazement for hours while her husband read the weekly newspaper aloud to her. And it was at these times he shone brightest as a wit.

Their eldest boy, Ehud, had run away from home. Nothing had been heard from him since then. Ever his mother grieved for him and prayed for his safety and for his return to her. So every now and then her husband—let's call him John Blank—would give a start of horror as he scanned the paper, and would shout:

"Gee! Just you listen to this piece of news off'n the front page, Arvilly!"

As she dropped her sewing, to hear the better, John Blank would begin his reading:

"Terrible Accident! Hundreds Perished by Getting Killed! Pennsylvania Train Tumbles Off'n the Track When Full of Folks! All of 'em Dies at Oncet! And These is the Names of Them That Was Killed: Ehud Blank and——"

The mother's heartbroken wail drowned out his voice at this point. Apron over her head, she would weep convulsively. Then when her merry spouse had

had his laugh out and had enjoyed her anguish to the full, he would say:

"Pshaw, now! I must get me a new pair of specs. I misread it wrong. The name was Eben Banks. But I thought as much as anything it was Ehud Blank."

In spite of many such happy reassurances, the poor woman would be quite as badly fooled the next time —perhaps a week later, perhaps in a month or more— when her husband read aloud the tale of some other mythical disaster—by sea, in a mine, in a hotel fire— and tacked Ehud Blank's name to the head of the casualty list.

Their Wanaque pastor used to rebuke John Blank for this foul cruelty toward his wife. But the dominie could not sweep the offender too searingly with the flame of his righteous wrath. This because the Blanks invited him to dinner every Sunday.

The poor clergyman received a negligible salary, when he received it at all. The only full meal he ate in the course of the week was that Sunday feast. There, urged hospitably by Mrs. Blank, he gorged like a man who is more than half starved. Which assuredly he was.

When at last he leaned back, glazed of eye and panting from sheer repletion, the good woman and he would exchange a brief dialogue—or ritual—that they continued unvaryingly every Sabbath, for a decade or more. Mrs. Blank would survey the stuffed parson and say solicitously:

"Why, Dominie, I'm afraid you don't like our victuals! You ain't made much of a meal."

And, as invariably, the preacher would reply:

"I thank you, I've et quite hearty."

One Sunday night, after such a midday gorge, the dominie died happily in his sleep; from acute indigestion.

I could write for fifty pages the tales—true, all of them, some of them worth telling—of my early neighbors and predecessors here and hereabout; and of the queer occurrences around Pompton. But I have told enough. If not more than enough. (Omitting the story of the aged North Jersey statesman who was obsessed by the notion that he was a postage stamp and went around weepingly beseeching strangers to lick him and paste him on a letter.)

In a wide field a tree grows as it wills to grow. In a tight clump its growth depends on that of the trees around it. Here, in olden days, there was elbow room for folk to develop their eccentricities as they might choose. In these modern decades, we are so crowded that our growth is circumscribed to a smugly standardized pattern.

Has this survey of the free-growing oldsters of Sunnybank's early times bored you? If it has, belatedly I ask your pardon for burdening you with it.

CHAPTER THIRTEEN

Mongrels All

ON MY desk here in my study lies a certified five-generation pedigree of one of my best dogs; Champion Sunnybank Thane, admittedly the foremost show-collie of his day. In the fifth generation there are thirty-two names; the names of his great-great-great-grandparents.

All thirty-two of Thane's great-great-great-grandparents were registered, in the infallible American Kennel Club Stud Book. Thus, the entire thirty-two were proven thoroughbreds. I owned many of them. I judged several others at various dogshows. I have seen all of them, during the past fifteen years or so.

I also have had thirty-two great-great-great-grandparents. Allowing the accepted average of three generations to a century, those thirty-two men and women were alive during the American Revolution. Indeed, their average birth date must have been somewhere around 1755.

Do I know who all, or even half, of my thirty-two

great-great-greats were? I do not. Nor do you know
who yours were. I don't even know who half of my
sixteen great-great-grandparents were; though they
must have been alive during part of the nineteenth
century.

Nor, I think, do you know who half of your own
great-greats were.

Champion Sunnybank Thane's five-generation pedigree is one hundred per cent certain. My own five-or-
even-four-generation pedigree is a mess.

So is yours.

It is humiliating. But it is true. Champion Sunnybank Thane was a proven thoroughbred; as far back
as the establishment of the Stud Book, and even further.

You and I are mongrels.

"Mongrel" is not a pretty word. But, for the moment, I can't think of a more accurate term to describe
us mixed-ancestored humans. Can you?

(Years ago, with the high-priced help of two professional genealogists, I wrote a preachment, setting
forth the incredible fact that all of us have had more
than forty million ancestors, since the time of William
the Conqueror; although there were not forty million
people in all Western Europe in the Conqueror's day.
Therein, I told of a Boston man who paid a group of
genealogists a big sum to trace his ancestry back, in
allegedly unbroken line, to Adam. If I remember
aright, he was in the one hundred and thirty-seventh
generation from Eve's mate.)

But there is no need to travel so far afield; or to

delve into the mists of the far past. The late eighteenth and the first half of the nineteenth centuries are not vaguely distant dates. And there is quite enough mongrelism in those two recent epochs for our purpose. So let's stick to them.

To begin with: you had two parents. Each of them had two parents. So you had four grandparents. In like sequence you had eight great-grandparents, sixteen great-great-grandparents, and thirty-two great-great-great-grandparents.

That brings you back to the fifth generation. And even that is further than you or I can travel with any accuracy.

I vision a reader snorting loudly at this point and declaiming:

"Rot! I know perfectly well who my great-great-great-grandfather was. The genealogy is as clear as crystal. He was Judge Eusebius Van Blanck, a Colonial Chief Justice and a signer of the Declaration of Independence. Through him, I can trace my family tree to burgomasters in Holland, two hundred years earlier. Yes, and Fredigonda, his wife, sprang from honored stock, in the Old Country. I can prove that my blood-lines are as pure as your Sunnybank collies'. You're talking nonsense, and I——"

Let me interrupt you, oh blue-blooded ancestor-worshiper, with a single query:

If only two of Champion Sunnybank Thane's thirty-two fifth-generation forebears could be proven to be purebred collies and if nobody knew to what breed or breeds the remaining thirty great-great-greats belonged, do you suppose he could be registered as a purebred collie?

Wouldn't he be the rankest of mongrels? All that could be established positively would be that he is one-sixteenth a collie.

I don't doubt you are descended from Judge Eusebius Van Blanck and from Fredigonda, his wife, and that they were all you say they were. But how about your thirty other great-great-greats who lived at the same time and who were every bit as much your direct ancestors as were the he-and-she Van Blancks?

Who were those thirty? How many of them can you name? If certain other fifth-generationers of yours are identifiable, the chances are a hundred to one that you cannot trace your line with any accuracy to more than four or six of them, at most.

Let us be foolishly liberal in our figures, and assume you can trace your descent from as many as eight of your great-great-greats—which almost no American can do.

Good! Then you can prove your descent from eight-thirty-seconds—one-fourth—of that generation. How about the other three-fourths; the other twenty-four great-great-greats who were just as much your ancestors as were Judge Eusebius Van Blanck and Fredigonda, his stodgy wife?

If I could prove Champion Sunnybank Thane had twenty-five per cent of good collie blood in his veins, would the American Kennel Club Stud Book have admitted his name to its close-guarded pages? Suppose I should say to the secretary of the club:

"Here is a five-generation pedigree I want certified. You will note there are only eight names in the fifth generation, where there ought to be thirty-two; and that there are corresponding blanks all down the list. But I know Champion Sunnybank Thane is at least twenty-five per cent a collie, whatever the other seventy-five per cent of his lineage may be. So please certify him as a purebred."

I should have to wait until doomsday for my certificate; besides stamping myself as an ignoramus in canine matters. But I would be doing nothing more foolish than were I to declare myself a thoroughbred on the strength of from two to eight known ancestors out of a requisite thirty-two.

Yet the members of the Society of the Cincinnati and the Colonial Dames and the Sons and Daughters of the American Revolution and of a dozen other famous genealogical organizations base their claims to admission on such 25 per cent-or-less justification.

That is not a wholly pleasant thought for those who belong. But there is comfort in it for the vast majority of us who do not belong.

It is high time that a dynamite cartridge of simple sanity be inserted under this ancestry fetish; high time for the truth to be told.

Let us get back to the aristocrat whose fifth generationers were Judge Eusebius Van Blanck and Fredigonda, his wife. While we are at it, let us grant him accurate knowledge of six more of his great-great-greats—a knowledge which not one person in fifty can claim.

That means three-fourths of his ancestors who lived during the American Revolution and somewhat later are wholly unknown to him.

He is making his brag on the strength of 25 per cent of the supposedly known truth. What about the rest of his forebears of that same day—the unknown 75 per cent of them? The 50 per cent of them, if you prefer. Who were they? *What* were they? Nobody knows. One very strong probability, however, sticks out like a sore thumb:

If they had been folk who amounted to anything, their children and their grandchildren would have remembered and passed along their name and their fame.

One cannot imagine, for example, a son of Patrick Henry or of Nathanael Greene or of Richard Stockton or of John Hancock failing to tell his children and his grandchildren anything about their illustrious progenitor.

One cannot imagine these children and grandchildren forgetting to mention his name to their own children and grandchildren. One cannot imagine the absence of some document or relic, to be handed down through the family; some effort to keep record of the straight line of descent from such an Immortal.

In fact, that is why Judge Eusebius Van Blanck is remembered. He was a major celebrity in his time. His descendants not only boasted about him, but they kept the records reasonably clear.

Which brings us back to my morbid statement that if the twenty-four unknown and forgotten great-great-greats had been worth embalming in family memories they would have been embalmed thus. Let's go a step further in the debunking process:

One does not talk about a parent or a grandparent who brought disgrace on the clan or who was of a so-called inferior race or who was worthless.

His or her name dies out quickly, in family annals. In other words, he or she becomes one of the unknown 75 per cent of the great-great-greats or even of the nineteenth century great-greats.

The name is obliterated. But his or her share in your ancestry cannot be obliterated.

Halfbreed Jake, the tramp, who was hanged for stealing food from the starving Continental army at Valley Forge, is just as much your great-great-great-grandfather as is Eusebius Van Blanck who signed the Declaration of Independence.

But Van Blanck's descendants wrapped Eusebius' name and deeds in a gold-stitched cloth and passed it on as an heirloom. That is how you know what relation he was to you.

Halfbreed Jake's beggar son may never have known his own sire's identity. If he did, it is not likely he told his children—perhaps illegitimate like himself—anything about the old blackguard. So, as the years dragged on, Eusebius was remembered. Jake was mercifully forgotten.

But you may inherit your rich brunette complexion quite as logically from halfbreed Jake's Indian or Negro mother as you inherit your aristocratic aquiline nose from the blue-blooded Eusebius. You can't accept one possibility without accepting both.

Yes, that may be an extreme case; but not necessarily so. Here is another instance, this time a true one; which helps to explain how an ancestral line may be untraceable (even though the lost one's strong traits and physical aspect may perhaps go on for centuries, side by side with those of more illustrious forebears):

Soon after the American Revolution, a handsome ne'er-do-well, who called himself Jesse Hawes, drifted into Dorchester, Massachusetts. He said he came from Maine, where "Hawes" was a somewhat common name of Isle of Wight English extraction, and that he had fought in the Revolution. He is described in an ancient letter as "of winning personality and handsome visage, but dissolute."

He wooed one Ann Pierce (pronounced "Purse)," the seventeen-year-old daughter of a Revolutionary colonel. Her father forbade him the house. He and Ann eloped and (presumably) were married.

Hawes was a chronic drunkard; as well as a chronic loafer. I know of no valid reason to believe his real name was Jesse or Hawes or that he actually came from Maine. One story he told his wife was that he was a foundling.

Presently he deserted Ann—after trying to stab her —and vanished. She came home to her father's house; there to bear her only child, a son—who was my mother's father.

So you see, in my own case, even in one of the two direct lines, my genealogy stops short in the fourth generation. For all I know, my great-great-great-grandfather (Jesse Hawes's father) may have been a Turk or a Chinaman or a Negro or George Washington or an Indian chief.

It is the same with all of us; to a greater or less degree—usually in a greater. Among our ancestry, in the fifth and the fourth and perhaps the third generations, there may well have been Indians (there is a larger mixture of Indian—as well as Negro—blood in us Americans than most people realize), Negroes, Hindus, Mormons, Catholics, Protestants, Jews and Quakers.

The most nearly pure blood lines, I believe, are to be found among the Jews. As for us Gentiles—

We don't know. We can only guess from certain physical and mental attributes which crop out unaccountably in family after family.

Among us, undoubtedly, are strains derived from every European country; and probably from Africa and Asia. There were illiterates and illegitimates in the throng; if nothing worse.

Our family trees in many instances may bear a humiliating likeness to a gallows tree.

We don't know. We know only that we are a mongrel mixture of a score of unidentified strains. Perhaps not one of us can claim Champion Sunnybank Thane's purity of blood.

I remember a man of noble French ancestry (on the known one-fourth side of his illustrious family) who had the features and the fleshless calves and the fingernails and much of the coloring of a Negro.

I knew a quadroon whose hair and beard were golden and whose eyes were blue; and who looked like a reincarnated Viking. A cleric uncle of my own had the features and complexion of a quarter-breed Indian.

Every now and then a "throwback," such as these, gives a more than vague hint at the wholesale mongrelism of us Americans. When I say "us Americans," I do so because we are the youngest of all races; and because, when our country was new, we were the most mixed lot of humans on earth. Folk of all races flocked here; to be absorbed in the melting pot.

There were fewer mixtures, in old-world countries; though there were plenty of them there, too. But people of those European and African and Asiatic blends swarmed into America; here to mingle and to interbreed with men and women whose ancestry was even more mixed. The result was the present-day American.

All this to show you that you have no right to make a fetish of your descent from Judge Eusebius Van

Blanck; and yet to ignore the origin of from 50 to 98 per cent of the rest of your make-up.

I have spoken of the thin aquiline nose which you inherit from old Eusebius; the exact counterpart of the nose in the Gilbert Stuart portrait of him which hangs in your dining room.

Why emphasize that nose, and yet slur over the features and characteristics which you inherit direct from such other equally near and equally prepotent forebears as Mike the Bite and Splitface Moll and perhaps (with a bar sinister) from Edgar Allan Poe and from Thomas Jefferson? Is it fair?

Some day, skim the works of Gregor Mendel; or at least an outline of the proven Mendelian Theory which accounts for unsmeared animal throwbacks dating sometimes to five generations or more ago.

For additional proof, you need look no further than into your own family connection; if you have one.

Here is a child who stands apart from his known ancestry as much as if he were a Japanese. Of old, these unaccountable "throwback" children were branded by the superstitious as "changelings."

The changeling in your own circle of relatives may be the check-forging son of a man of God. He may be the incurably lazy son of two thrifty and tirelessly industrious parents.

He may be a second Napoleon Bonaparte (and perhaps many of us are descended from the Bonapartes, several sexful members of whose family honored our country with their presence during their exile-years);

or he may be a lad who has risen shiningly to holiness from the family muck. Or he may drag a shiningly clean family down into the mire.

He is a throwback. But to whom? God knows. To one of your twenty-four or thirty-two unknown great-great-greats; or to one of your often unknown sixteen (or fewer) great-greats who lived less than a century ago.

It is wholly possible that your elder son may have inherited Judge Eusebius Van Blanck's aquiline nose and even the old jurist's taste for the law. He may well be a five-generation throwback, in several ways.

But where did your second-born son get his heart-deep craving to be a painter or a poet or a concert pianist or a crook or a dilettante in ceramics—he whose known forebears were all hard-headed business men, unimaginative and upright and starkly practical?

He didn't evolve those tastes from nothingness. Just as strong an ancestral urge as called your elder son to law summoned his younger brother to the arts or to the gutter.

Perhaps a painter or a scribbler or an actor proved more than resistibly fascinating to your wedded grand-mother or great-grandmother.

Perhaps in legitimate descent, through one of the twenty-four-to-thirty-two unknown ancestral channels, an artistic forebear left his prepotent traits to crop out intact—like red hair—several generations later.

There was scant honor or wealth here in America for such Bohemians, in colonial or early national decades. Well may their strain have become forgotten.

In my Sunnybank collie kennels, again and again, there is born a pup which is a 100 per cent throwback to some ancestor of five generations ago. Not only in looks but in character.

His aspect and his nature have slept for generations and then have emerged intact.

Champion Sunnybank Thane (to cite only one case) was physically and mentally Champion Sunnybank Sigurd (Treve), a direct ancestor who died years before Thane was born.

I know whence these throwback pups glean their cosmos. The merest span of years separates them from their fifth-generation ancestors—Sunnybank dogs which were my pals and which I studied as never did I study a school lesson.

But I don't know where I myself got certain overmastering traits which have shaped my whole life and character and which I can't identify with those of anyone in my known heritage.

My mother, for example, was only five feet four inches tall. She came from a line of short or medium-sized folk. My father was well under six feet tall; and he was the tallest of his kin.

At sixteen, I stood six feet two and a half inches in my bare feet; and I was on the road to weighing well above two hundred pounds.

To what unknown ancestral giant did I throw back?

My mother, bred of a race of stolid business men and clergymen, could not free herself from the yearn-

ing for a writer's career; even though in her youth
it was deemed unworthy for a woman to take up
literature for a livelihood.

To what eighteenth-century unknown or left-
handed scribbling ancestor was she a throwback? Who
can guess?

I mention these personal matters; not that they can
be of any interest, but because they prove my point and
because I can attest to their truth.

Barring the occasional throwback, all of us are
blends of—we don't know what. Most of us (except
the Jews) are at least three-fourths of unknown descent;
we who call our ancestry flawless.

You and I, in short, are mongrels. We have not the
remotest idea from what mixture of human races we
spring. We may be, by some miracle, pure Nordic or
pure Latin. But the chances are a thousand to one
against it. We are a jumble: Jew, Gentile, Aryan,
Caucasian, and everything else.

Why does nobody know the vari-breed ancestry
of the average mongrel dog? Because the cur's ancestors weren't worth recording and their tangled
pedigrees could not be filed in the Stud Book. These
dogs were not eligible to registration. Nobody bothered to keep track of the mongrel's family tree.

Nobody bothered to keep track of my family tree
or of yours; except in from two to eight thirty-seconds
of its many branches, at most.

Your mongrel cur traces back to as many blue-
ribbon thoroughbreds as do you and I; and quite as

directly. The rest, with both the dogs and ourselves, is just a scrambled snarl of mixed blood lines whose very memory is quickly lost.

Should we not remember this with comfort, rather than with shame? Especially next time we hear a friend vaunt his election to some genealogical society to which we apparently are not eligible?

He has other ancestors through whom he might equally be elected to a jail term.

There is no such thing as a family tree. At best, there is only a half-handful of mixed twigs. The bulk of the tree is (luckily) a solveless mystery.

Yes, my Sunnybank collies have an immeasurable advantage over me. They are thoroughbred. I am not.

Neither are you.

CHAPTER FOURTEEN

Fair Ellen of Sunnybank

SUNNYBANK FAIR ELLEN is dead.

For twelve years she lived under a suspended death sentence; a sentence never put into effect.

She was a strange little golden collie; a dog that never saw a glimmer of light. She was born blind—as are all dogs—and she remained blind throughout more than a decade of such gay happiness as falls to the lot of few collies or humans.

I don't know how many people came to Sunnybank, first and last, to see our queer little blind dog—daughter of Treve—and to marvel at her jollity and at her uncanny cleverness. But the number ran high into the thousands. Many persons—myself among them—have written about her. (In my book, *The Way of a Dog*, I tell the tale of the first part of her life far more fully than I can tell it here.)

In her way she became something of a celebrity; though she did not know it. Any more than she knew she was blind. Yet she knew that she was happy and that everybody made much of her; and that the other collies were gentle with her, even in their roughest romps.

As when great old Sunnybank Gray Dawn died, five years ago, I forbade anyone at Sunnybank to speak of Ellen's death; during such time as it still could come under the head of news. I didn't want reporters sent out here to ask well-meant questions about our sightless chum.

Most of Ellen's horde of friends will read now, for the first time, of her passing.

I said Ellen lived for twelve years under a suspended sentence. Let me explain.

When the other pups of the litter opened their eyes, anywhere from nine to fourteen days after they were born, Fair Ellen's lids remained tight shut. A week or so later, they opened; but they were white-filmed.

I sent for a vet, then for another, and at last for an expert from Cornell University's veterinary school. In turn these experts examined the fluffy gold puppy. Their reports were alike:

The white film could be—and was—removed. But there were dead optic nerves behind it. The dog never could see. She had nothing to see with.

There seemed to be but one thing to do; one sane and merciful way to solve the sorry problem. I loaded my pistol, to put her out of her misery.

It was the Mistress who intervened, by reminding me that Fair Ellen had no "misery" to be put out of;

that she was the gladdest and liveliest and most fun-loving member of that historic litter of glad and lively and fun-loving collie babies.

The Mistress begged that Ellen be allowed to stay alive, for as long a time as she might continue to be happy; as long as the life which had cheated her so cruelly should keep on giving her a good time.

"She is happy," pleaded the Mistress. "Is there so much happiness in the world, that you must destroy part of it?"

So the sentence was suspended. And never thereafter was there reason to execute it.

I watched closely for the reprieved collie's first sign of discomfort or of sadness. Meanwhile I did what I could for her well-being. Then it was that I began to notice certain oddities about her. For instance:

When the six-weeks-old family of pups were taken from the broodnest and turned loose in the huge "puppy-yard," they began at once to explore this immense territory of theirs.

At almost every fifth step, Fair Ellen's hobbyhorse gallop would bring her into sharp contact with the food dish, the drinking pan, the fence wires, a post of the raised sleeping quarters or the trunk of one of the enclosure's shade trees or some other obstacle which her four brothers avoided with ease.

Always she would pick herself up after such collision, with tail wagging and fat golden body wriggling as if at some rare joke. Some of these bumps must have been bruisingly painful to the pudgy youngster. But not once did she whimper; nor did she fail to greet each mishap merrily.

Then I noticed that never did she collide with the same obstacle a second time. Coming close to food dish or tree trunk or the like, she would make a careful detour.

In less than a week she had learned the location of every obstacle, big or small, in the yard. She could traverse the whole space at a gallop—interspersed with swirling detours—without once colliding with a thing.

Perhaps this does not seem to you a clever or an unusual stunt. Very good. Make mental note of the position of any one object—not a whole yardful of them—at perhaps twenty feet away from you. Then shut your eyes and walk quickly toward it.

If you can figure out how to make precisely the right-sized detour at precisely the right place, in order to avoid bumping into the object you are walking toward, then you have far more distance sense than I have; or than had scores of my successive guests who, seeing Ellen do this, tried blindfold to achieve the same trick.

It simply couldn't be done.

Yet the blind puppy taught herself to do it with no difficulty at all. Remember, her world was black dark. Remember, too, that this darkness was strewn with things against which she was likely to bump.

In some wholly unexplainable way, she found out

for herself just where each and every one of these
stumbling blocks was, and just when and how far to
detour around them.

It was not a spectacular stunt, perhaps. But to me
it seemed—and still seems—a minor miracle.

It was the same, presently, when I took her out of
the puppy-yard for an hour or so a day, for a walk
with me. I wanted to try an experiment—to see if
Ellen could carry that amazing distance-gauging gift
into the real outdoors.

She could.

Our first few walks around the grounds and the
stables were fraught with collision after collison for
the poor little dog. Into tree trunks and into building
corners and posts and benches and shrubbery clumps
she bungled. But—as in her own yard—never into
the same one a second time.

Bit by bit I enlarged our daily rambles. I was teaching her the lay of the whole forty-acre Place. And
never did pupil learn faster.

Numberless friends of ours can testify that within
a few weeks Ellen could gallop all over the lawns
and the orchard and the oak groves at top speed.
That she could even canter along close to the many-
angled kennel yards and stable buildings without a
single collision. To the day of her death, twelve years
later, she still could do this.

It was on one of these educational rambles of ours
that her fast-running feet carried her into the lake. It

was her first contact with a body of water larger than her drinking pan; and her impetus carried her out into it, up to her neck.

With a gay bark she began to swim. Most dogs, on their first immersion into lake or river, swim high and awkwardly. Ellen did not.

She took to the water with perfect ease, as to a familiar element. She swam out for perhaps a hundred feet. Then she hesitated, lifting her head as though to catch some familiar sound or scent to guide her.

I called her by name. She turned and swam back to shore, to my feet; steering her sightless course wholly by memory of my single call.

To me, that also seemed something rather out of the ordinary. Thereafter, her daily swim was one of Ellen's chief joys.

I noted something else, in my hours of unobserved watching:

That was one of the roughest and most bumptious yardfuls of collie pups, out of the hundreds of litters I have bred and raised—Sigurdson, Cavalier, Explorer, Jamie, and the rest. Their play was strenuous almost to the point of mayhem.

Yet when Fair Ellen joined in their romps, as always she did when she was in the yard with them, they did not roll her over nor sling her around as they did one another. They were absurdly gentle, awkwardly gentle; very evidently seeking not to hurt her.

In some mystic fashion the young collie ruffians seemed to understand that she was not as they were.

So long as she lived, that was the attitude taken toward her by several generations of Sunnybank dogs of both sexes.

There was only one exception. That was when a hot-tempered female collie flew at her, snarling, when Ellen was about five years old. Before the bitch's teeth could close on Ellen, three other female dogs had borne the aggressor to the ground and were trying industriously to thrash her to death.

A vet who specialized in eye troubles told me there was no reason to think Fair Ellen's blindness would be carried on in any puppies she might have. He was right. She had several litters of pups, during her twelve years; and every pup was of perfect sight and perfect health in every way.

Because she had such splendid pups, I received offers of much cash, from time to time, for her; from professional breeders. I refused them all. In a strange place, she might well have become confused or unhappy; and some swine of a kennelman might have been unkind to her.

Besides, as I told you, she was under suspended sentence. I was waiting for a time to come when she should grow mopey and lose some of her odd delight in life. Meanwhile, it was up to me to do what I could for her, to put off as long as might be that seemingly inevitable day.

And she was having a glorious time. She invented queer little games, which she played, for the most part, alone.

One of these was to listen for the winnowing of homecoming pigeons' wings. The birds might be flying so high as to make this winnowing inaudible to human ears. But Ellen heard.

Always she would set off in pursuit, running at full speed directly under the pigeons, swerving and circling when they swerved and circled; guided wholly by that miraculous hearing of hers—the same sense of ear which told her from exactly what direction a storm was coming up, long before the first growls of thunder were audible to any of the rest of us.

She had some nameless sense, beyond acute hearing, too. I don't know what it was. But by reason of it I have seen her stop dead short, not six inches from a wall or a solid fence toward which she had been galloping at express-train speed.

(I am told blind humans, some of them, have this mystic sense.)

I sat up with her, all night, when her first puppies were born. There were nine of them. She did not seem to have the remotest idea what or whose they were.

The night was bitter cold. Ellen for once in her life was jumpy with taut nerves. For many hours, I had a man's size job keeping her quiet and keeping the nine babies from dying of chill.

At last, long after sunrise, Ellen began groping about her with her nose, snuggling the puppies close to her furrily warm underbody and making soft crooning noises at them.

Then I knew my task was ended; and that her abnormally keen ears had caught old Dame Nature's all-instructive whisper. Thereafter, she was an ideal little mother.

As the years crawled on, Ellen's jollity and utter joy in life did not abate. Gradually her muzzle began to whiten. Gradually the sharp teeth dulled from long contact with gnawed bones. Her daily gallops grew shorter. But ever the spirit of puppy fun flared forth as when she was young.

She would romp with me, wildly, as always she had done. The seemingly noiseless slipping of my fingers into the side pocket of my leather coat, where always lie a handful of animal crackers, would bring her rushing up to me from many feet away; in gay expectation of the treat.

One after the other, two of her brothers, Sunnybank Sigurdson and Sunnybank Explorer, won their championships in the show ring; and gained national fame among dog-fanciers.

Another brother of hers, Sunnybank Cavalier, won a series of sensational show victories.

All this time Sunnybank Fair Ellen, most beautiful of the litter, stayed quietly at home. For the American Kennel Club wisely forbids the showing of a blind dog.

One by one these renowned brothers of hers waxed old, and died. But Ellen lived on.

Champion Sunnybank Sigurdson—whose head-study adorned at least one government pamphlet, as the

Ideal Collie—was smitten by a malady which the best vets could not even name, much less cure.

It was a form of paralysis which, when Sigurdson was ten years old, crippled his hindquarters and struck him blind.

Unlike his blind sister, Sigurdson was in great and increasing mental misery. And the pistol I had loaded a decade earlier for Fair Ellen was then reloaded.

Many breeders kill dogs that are no longer of use to them; or else sell them to unsuspecting strangers. At Sunnybank's kennels we don't make our living that way. An outworn collie is allowed to live on, in happy laziness, until life becomes unbearable to him or to her.

Then, the swiftest end is the kindest end. Not by chloroform, from whose effects too many dogs have recovered, five feet underground, there to smother to death; but by a high-power bullet, rightly placed.

Now life had become unbearable to our gorgeous ten-year-old Champion Sunnybank Sigurdson. And there was but one thing to do.

Sparingly and seldom do I give lumps of sugar to our dogs. For sugar is bad for every one of their forty-two teeth. And a dog's digestive apparatus has no way of disposing of sweets.

But, after show victories and at other gala times, a lump of sugar had been tossed to Sigurdson. He loved sugar better than anything and everything else on earth.

So, one morning in 1932, a pound of cut-up porterhouse steak was set before the blind and paralyzed old champion. He ate it with dainty relish.

Then, into his food dish was poured a whole pound of lump sugar.

It was pathetic to watch his unbelieving delight as he nosed out and ate not merely the single morsel of this delicacy which sometimes had been apportioned to him in former days; but lump after lump. Dozens and scores of delicious lumps of sugar.

With the zest of an epicure he chewed and swallowed them, one after the other. Long and slowly he ate. It was his crowning moment. He thrilled to it.

As he swallowed the last lump of the entire pound and bent his sightless head to grope for another, the merciful bullet went through his brain.

He did not know what had happened. His death was instant and painless; in the midst of the most stupendously happy feast he ever had known.

Laugh at me, if you like, for that foolish waste of sugar and meat on a doomed dog to whom the food could do no lasting good.

I grant it was maudlin. And I am not interested in anyone's opinion of it—or of me. My old chum died supremely happy; he to whom happiness had long been a stranger.

Let's get back to Fair Ellen, shall we—to the dog whose destined bullet went astray and killed her once vigorous brother?

On the afternoon of July First, 1933, Ellen and I went for one of our daily rambles—walks whose length was cut down nowadays by reason of her increasing age.

She was in dashing high spirits, and she danced all around me. We had a jolly hour, loafing about the lawns together. Then, comfortably tired, she trotted into her yard and lay down for her usual late afternoon nap.

When I passed by, an hour later, she was still lying stretched out there in the shade. But, for the first time in twelve years, the sound of my step failed to bring her eagerly to her feet to greet me. This was so unusual that I went into the yard and bent down to see what was amiss.

Quietly, without pain, still happy, she had died in her sleep.

I can think of a thousand worse ways of saying good-bye to this thing we call Life.

THE END